WHERE SECOND CHANCES BEGIN

WHERE SECOND CHANCES BEGIN

PREQUEL

THE LIVES WE CHOOSE

LIZ BROWN

TREASURE STONE PRESS

*For those who feel love has passed you by,
love can find you late.*

"We would be together and have our books and at night be warm in bed together with the windows open and the stars bright."

— ERNEST HEMINGWAY

CHAPTER 1

MICHAEL

The market was still coming to life when Michael Holmes arrived.

He liked it best like this, before voices became loud and overlapping, the air filled with the clink of coins and the polite chaos of people deciding what to buy and what to put back. The stalls stood half-open like books with their pages not yet turned, canvas awnings damp with morning dew and crates stacked in rows.

Michael nodded at the man from the fruit stand, who lifted a hand without fully looking up from his apples. He returned the gesture to a woman he'd seen here for years; she sold soaps wrapped in decorative brown paper and always wore gloves no matter the season. Familiar faces and familiar routines. The comfort of it sat in his chest the way his jumper sat on his shoulders: simple, dependable and warm.

Michael didn't hurry. He never had, not really. Years in the post office had taught him there was no point rushing a letter that would arrive when it arrived. The world moved at its own pace; all you could do was try to move kindly within it.

At the end of the row of stalls, he reached the shared tables. They were simple things, weathered wood, bolted benches, and the edges worn smooth by elbows and time. Someone had carved a heart into the tabletop years ago, then scratched it out, then carved it again. Love, Michael thought, had a habit of returning to the same place.

He chose the table that faced the river path, though the Ouse itself was hidden behind buildings and the rise of the street. Still, he liked knowing it was there, sliding along beyond sight, doing what it had always done.

He set his cup down and sat.

The coffee was from one of the pop-up ones that came and went like migrating birds. It wasn't as good as the coffee he remembered from the little café Janet used to like, but it was hot, and that counted for something on a morning like this. He cupped his hands around it, feeling the heat seep into his fingers.

Around him, the noises of the market waking for the day filled his ears: a van backed into place, beeping as it reversed, someone laughed and a dog shook itself hard enough to rattle its lead.

Michael watched the market come to life. For decades he'd watched people step up to his counter with envelopes and parcels and expressions they didn't know they were wearing.

He took a slow sip and let the warmth settle.

The chair across from him was empty, and the other tables were slowly filling with couples enjoying their morning together.

He didn't linger on the thought; he didn't like the

feeling of lingering on things that could not be changed. Janet had been gone long enough that grief no longer felt sharp; it lived in him like an old ache that flared when the weather changed. Some mornings he woke and still reached, half-asleep, toward a space that was no longer filled, but most mornings he did not.

Today, he only looked at the empty chair across from him and then looked away.

A woman approached the table with a cup in her hand.

Michael didn't recognize her, which was unusual. He recognized most people who kept the market as part of their routine. But then, routines changed. People came and went. He'd spent his life handling departures in the form of forwarding addresses and redirection slips; he knew better than most how easily a person could vanish from one daily world and appear in another.

She paused at the end of the table.

"Do you mind if I sit here?" she asked, touching the back of the chair across from him.

Her voice was warm and cheerful without being loud about it. Like sunlight in winter that didn't pretend it was summer.

Michael lifted his gaze.

She was around his age, maybe a little younger, with silver threaded through brown hair that had been pulled back in a practical twist. Colorful bracelets circled one wrist with bright beads that looked like they'd been chosen on purpose, not to match anything, but simply because they pleased her. Her other wrist had several bracelets with little silver charms that sparkled in the sunlight.

She held her cup as if it belonged there, as if she belonged there.

Michael blinked once, then offered the chair with a small nod.

"No," he said. "Go ahead."

Relief flickered across her face, quick as a match strike. She sat, careful not to bump the table, and set her cup down.

"Thank you. I really needed to sit down." she said and smiled at him as if they were already acquainted.

Michael found himself returning it.

"You're welcome."

She took a sip, sighed, and glanced down the row of stalls as if greeting the morning.

"I always forget how cool it is in the morning until I'm actually here," she said.

Michael huffed a soft laugh.

"York does that," he agreed. "It looks charming, and then it reminds you it's made of stone and history."

Her smile widened. "Exactly."

She stirred her tea thoughtfully.

Michael watched the small movement of her hand and felt a strange flicker of familiarity he couldn't quite place.

Not recognition exactly.

Just the faint sense that he had once sat across from her before, somewhere quieter, somewhere long ago, watching that same careful concentration.

Michael was aware of something in himself shifting, small, almost imperceptible. The way a door might settle an inch wider when you didn't even realize it was closed.

He took another sip of coffee.

The woman turned her head slightly, studying him in a way that didn't feel like scrutiny but curiosity.

"I'm Abbie Payne," she said.

Michael set his cup down carefully before answering.

"Michael," he replied. "Michael Holmes."

"Michael Holmes," she repeated, "Nice to meet you."

He nodded, "Nice to meet you too."

Abbie lifted her cup. "Here's to staying warm," she said.

Michael lifted his in return. "And to not letting the weather win."

She laughed, and for the first time in a very long while, he found himself hoping the conversation wouldn't end, and for reasons he couldn't quite explain, that felt like a very good start to the day.

CHAPTER 2

ABBIE

Abbie Payne rarely sat at someone else's table.

But the man sitting alone at a table near the corner caught her attention. Perhaps it was simply that the morning felt too pleasant to spend entirely alone and she did want to sit and enjoy her tea.

You're being ridiculous, she thought.

He was only a stranger enjoying his morning coffee.

If he preferred the chair to remain empty, he could easily say so.

With that quiet reasoning, Abbie weaved her way through the full tables and rested her hand lightly on the back of the chair.

"Do you mind if I sit here?" she asked.

"No," he said. "Go ahead."

She pulled the chair out and settled herself across from him and took a sip of her tea. It was stronger than she expected, which she took as a good sign.

She wrapped both hands around the cup and let the

warmth settle into her fingers while the morning market gathered itself into motion. There was something comforting about arriving before everything was fully underway, the sense that the day was still deciding what it might become.

Across from her, Michael Holmes sat with the kind of stillness she associated with people who had learned not to rush anything that mattered.

She had noticed that immediately, and noticed, too, that he had looked at the empty chair before she spoke, as if acknowledging its emptiness before inviting it to change. That detail stayed with her.

She took a small sip of tea and tried not to smile to herself, which only made her smile more.

"Well," she said lightly, "this is nicer than sitting on my own pretending to read a book I'm not actually reading."

Michael's mouth tipped upward.

"I've done that," he said. "Though with newspapers instead of books."

"Newspapers are worse," Abbie replied. "They expect you to frown."

"That they do."

The conversation settled into place between them, not hurried, not fragile. Abbie recognized the feeling immediately, the easy rhythm she used to see when two children who had never met discovered they could build something together out of wooden blocks without arguing over who got which color.

She set her cup down carefully.

"I come here most Thursdays," she said. "Habit, I suppose."

Michael nodded once. "I come most days."

"Most days," she repeated, glancing around the market

as if recalibrating her understanding of it. "That explains why you look like you belong."

He seemed amused by that. "I'm not sure I do."

"You do," Abbie said simply.

She noticed the black marker tucked behind his ear then. The sight made her think immediately of classroom whiteboards and spelling exercises, and of encouragement written large enough for a child to believe.

"You're prepared," she said, nodding toward them.

Michael reached up, touched one as if confirming its presence, and gave a small shrug.

"Habit," he said again.

Abbie liked that word in his voice. It didn't sound like resignation. It sounded like steadiness.

A gull swooped low over the market, drawing her gaze upward. The sky had brightened into that pale winter blue that never quite promised warmth but still suggested possibility.

She loved mornings like this.

Edward had loved them too.

The thought arrived without warning but without sharpness. Just a memory stepping quietly into the room.

Edward with his gardening gloves tucked into his back pocket. Edward insisting that tea tasted better outside, no matter the weather. Edward laughing when she'd tried to correct his pronunciation of "hyacinth" and failed.

She breathed once, steady.

Michael took a sip of coffee, giving her the space without appearing to do so. She recognized that kind of kindness instantly, the sort that didn't ask questions unless invited.

She appreciated it more than she could say.

"So," she said after a moment, tilting her head slightly,

"are you a York native, Michael Holmes, or did the city adopt you later in life?"

"Later," he answered. "After retirement."

"Ah." She nodded approvingly. "A sensible time to relocate. Less paperwork."

That earned her a soft laugh.

"And you?" he asked.

"Mostly local," she said. "Close enough to visit often."

She didn't elaborate. Not yet. Conversations were like lessons, you didn't give all the information at once. You let understanding build piece by piece.

A dog trotted past, tail wagging with such determination that Abbie smiled again.

Michael noticed.

"You like dogs," he said.

"I like enthusiasm," she replied.

"Fair."

The market had grown louder now as vendors called greetings and a coffee grinder whirred somewhere behind them. Abbie found herself studying Michael again.

"You're very good at mornings," she said suddenly.

He blinked.

"I beg your pardon?"

"You sit like someone who understands them," she clarified. "Some people fight mornings and look like they want to go back to bed. You don't."

Michael considered that, then shrugged lightly.

"They come whether you fight them or not."

Abbie laughed again, softer this time. "That is a fact."

"That sounds like something a teacher would say," he added.

"I was a primary school teacher" she replied, remembering the chatter of little voices coming into the classroom each morning

"Explains the bracelets," Michael said.

Abbie glanced down at the little charm bracelets on her wrist and smiled.

"They were gifts," she said. "End-of-term traditions."

"That's a good tradition."

"It is. I like how they bring back memories of my students."

They fell into silence again, but this time it felt like shared space rather than empty space. Abbie found she didn't mind it. Silence had frightened her once, after Edward died, and she hadn't known how to fill it. Now it felt comfortable and more like breathing room.

Michael finished his coffee slowly.

Abbie watched the steam from her tea thin and disappear.

"I should let you enjoy your time," she said at last, though she didn't feel particularly eager to leave.

Michael nodded.

"Will you be here the same time tomorrow?" he asked, almost casually.

The question warmed her more than the tea had.

"I think so," Abbie said.

"I'll save the chair for you then."

She stood, sliding her chair back carefully. Michael rose halfway, then sat again, as if unsure whether standing was necessary. The small awkwardness made her fond of him immediately.

"Nice to meet you, Michael Holmes," she said again.

"And you, Abbie."

She turned toward the path leading away from the

market, bracelets chiming softly against one another as she walked.

Halfway down the row of stalls, she realized she was humming but she didn't stop.

And though she did not look back, she carried with her the quiet certainty that tomorrow morning, the chair across from Michael Holmes would not be empty.

CHAPTER 3

MICHAEL

Michael did not usually have to think about the walk home. He had walked it often enough that his feet knew the rhythm without instruction. It was not far, just a handful of streets, a crossing where the traffic lights took longer than seemed necessary, and a narrow row of shops that smelled faintly of bread even when the bakery was closed.

Today, however, the walk felt... different, like he was slightly out of step with himself.

He kept his hands in his coat pockets as he walked, fingers brushing the smooth plastic barrel of another marker he'd absentmindedly slipped there. He hadn't meant to do that, but his habit of carrying small tools lingered from years behind the post office counter, pencils, paperclips, small pieces of paper, and other things that made small tasks easier.

He wondered, briefly, what he might need a marker for on the walk home.

The thought made him smile.

At the crossing, he stopped beside a young man pushing a bicycle. The man tapped one foot impatiently while watching the red light, as if impatience might persuade it to change. Michael watched too, but without urgency.

The light turned green when it was ready.

On the other side, a bus rumbled past, carrying a row of faces in its windows, some tired, some blank, and one person laughing into a phone. Michael found himself looking for Abbie's reflection among them, though he knew she had walked in the opposite direction.

He told himself he was only noticing the morning more carefully than usual.

That was all.

He turned onto his street. The houses stood shoulder to shoulder, brick and stone, with blue recycling bin lined up along the sides. Someone's curtains had been left open, revealing a kitchen where a kettle steamed beneath a window. Ordinary life, continuing as it always did.

Michael unlocked the front door to his flat and stepped inside, greeted with its familiar stillness. He hung his coat on the hook by the door, the same hook it had occupied for years, and set his keys in the shallow ceramic dish Janet had once chosen at a charity shop because she liked the painted daisies around the rim.

He paused there for a moment, listening to the silence; then he moved into the kitchen. The kettle did not need to be filled, but he filled it anyway. The motion was comforting, water running, lid closing, and clicking down the switch. He set his empty cup in the sink and rinsed it, though it was already clean.

On the small table by the window sat the morning post

he had collected earlier, a circular from the council and a letter addressed to a neighbor who had moved months ago.

He turned the letter over in his hands. Forwarding addresses were no longer his responsibility, but the instinct to correct a wrong address remained strong. He set it aside to return later.

He poured himself a cup of tea he did not particularly want and carried it into the sitting room. His chair by the window creaked as he sat. Across from it, Janet's chair remained where it had always been, not preserved deliberately, but simply never moved.

The house did not feel lonely but felt complete in a quieter way than it once had.

Michael sipped the tea and found himself replaying the morning without meaning to, thinking about the tinkling sound of Abbie's bracelets, her laugh, and the way she had said *You're very good at mornings.*

He had never thought of himself that way.

He looked down at the tea in his hands and realized he was smiling.

That surprised him enough to make him laugh, softly, to himself.

"Well," he said aloud, the word settling easily into the room.

The clock on the mantel ticked forward.

Outside, a car door slammed and somewhere nearby, a radio played faintly through an open window. The world continued its ordinary business.

Michael stood and carried his cup back to the kitchen.

On the counter sat a small notepad he used for grocery lists. He picked it up without thinking and uncapped the marker he'd brought home. The tip hovered above the paper. He didn't know why he was doing this, but he wrote anyway.

Still time.

The words looked slightly crooked in his careful block lettering. Michael studied them for a moment, then nodded once, as if confirming something to himself, and left the note on the counter where he would see it.

He rinsed his cup, dried his hands, and moved back into the quiet rhythm of his day with the faint sense that tomorrow morning might arrive with a reason to return to the market a little earlier than usual.

CHAPTER 4

Abbie did not usually hurry home from the market. There were small detours she liked to take, a walk past the florist's window, a pause at the corner where the bakery sometimes set out day-old loaves, and slow looks at the charity shops' displays that rarely changed but always felt worth checking.

Today, she found herself walking a little more directly than usual.

Her bracelets clinked softly together as she adjusted the strap of her bag on her shoulder. The sound had followed her for years now, a small, cheerful accompaniment to ordinary movement. She had never intended to keep wearing them after she stopped teaching, but they had become part of her in a way she hadn't expected.

A group of schoolchildren passed her on the pavement, loud with the particular energy of midmorning freedom. One of them dropped a mitten and didn't notice.

"Excuse me," Abbie called gently.

The child turned, eyes wide, and she held out the mitten like a small treasure being returned.

"Thank you," the child said, shyly.

"You're welcome," Abbie replied, smiling in the way that had once calmed nervous first-day students.

The group moved on, voices fading.

Abbie stood for a moment, watching them go.

Edward had loved seeing children on their way to school. He used to say it reminded him that the world kept renewing itself whether people noticed or not.

She smiled at the memory and continued walking.

Her house was small but bright, with a narrow garden that did its best despite the stubbornness of the soil. She let herself in, set her bag on the chair by the door, and paused in the familiar quiet.

She moved into the kitchen and set the kettle on, though she still had half a cup of tea left in the paper cup she'd carried home. Old habits from years of making tea for others were difficult to break and she was ready for a second cup.

While the water heated, she opened the window a few inches. Cold air slipped inside, carrying the faint smell of damp pavement and distant bread.

Her humming returned as the kettle clicked off. She poured water into a clean cup, adding a teabag. On the kitchen table sat a stack of folded papers, lesson plans from another life, kept for reasons she never fully examined. She slid a chair back and sat, resting her hands around the warm cup.

Michael Holmes.

She said the name silently, testing it the way she once tested new vocabulary words with her students.

There was something about him.

She thought about the way he had waited a moment before saying his name, as if names deserved care.

That detail pleased her.

She reached across the table and pulled the back of an old grocery list toward her. Without thinking much about it, she found a pen and wrote:

Market — Thursday morning.

Then she added, beneath it:

Michael.

She looked at the words for a moment, then laughed softly at herself.

"Well," she said to the empty kitchen, "that's new."

The clock on the wall ticked its steady rhythm.

She sipped the fresh tea and let her thoughts drift.

Edward's face came easily, his patient smile, the way he used to lean against the doorframe while she graded papers at the table. Grief still lived in the house, but it no longer startled her when it appeared. It moved like a familiar guest, quiet and respectful.

She did not feel guilty for the warmth she'd felt at the market. That surprised her a little, but not in an unpleasant way.

She rose from the table and carried her cup to the sink, rinsing it carefully. Sunlight had begun to push through the clouds, touching the edge of the counter and the small jar of wooden spoons beside the stove.

Abbie dried her hands on a dish towel and glanced at the paper again.

Market — Thursday morning. Michael.

The sight of it made her smile, not broadly, but just enough to feel the corners of her mouth lift.

She folded the paper once and tucked it beneath the edge of the sugar bowl, where it would not be lost. Then she moved into the sitting room and opened a book she did not immediately read.

Outside, somewhere down the street, a door closed and footsteps passed, and the day stretched ahead in its ordinary shape.

Yet beneath the calm, Abbie felt the quiet anticipation of tomorrow morning, like the first page of a lesson she had not yet begun but already knew she would enjoy teaching.

And though she did not say it aloud, she knew that she would return to the market in the morning, and not just for the tea.

CHAPTER 5

MICHAEL

Michael arrived at the market earlier than usual the next morning.

He noticed this only after he had already sat down.

It was the same table, the same chair, and the same slow arrangement of morning sounds. He set his coffee in front of him and rested his hands around it, letting the heat seep into his fingers.

The chair across from him was empty, but not in the same way it had been yesterday. Today, he hoped Abbie would be back to fill it.

He watched the path leading between the stalls without appearing to do so. A woman with a shopping trolley passed, then a man carrying bread wrapped in paper, and then a pair of tourists consulting a map.

Michael took a sip of coffee.

The air smelled faintly of roasted beans and damp wood.

"You're early today."

He looked up, startled.

Abbie stood beside the table, tea in hand, bracelets shimmering in the morning light.

Michael felt the smallest lift of relief, so small it might have been mistaken for nothing at all.

"So are you," he said.

She sat, the chair legs scraping softly against the stone.

"I wondered if you might be here," she admitted.

"I wondered the same."

They exchanged a brief smile, comfortable already.

Abbie blew across the surface of her tea before taking a careful sip. Michael noticed her order written on the cup, milk, no sugar, and filed the detail away without thinking about why.

"It's cold again," she said.

"York hasn't changed overnight," he replied.

"It's disappointing."

He chuckled.

For a moment they simply sat, watching the market assemble itself, a man unloaded trays of rolls at a baked goods stall, while someone argued cheerfully about the price of tomatoes.

Michael found the quiet between them easier today.

"Did you teach nearby?" he asked after a while.

Abbie nodded. "Yes, the primary school. For many years."

"And you?" she asked. "What did you do before you became very good at mornings?"

"Postmaster."

Her expression brightened immediately.

"Oh, I like that," she said. "You must have known everyone."

"Most of them," Michael replied. "Or their parcels, at least."

Abbie laughed.

"That explains it," she said.

"Explains what?"

"You notice things. Teachers do that too. We have to."

Michael considered this.

"I suppose we both spent our lives paying attention," he said.

"That sounds right."

A brief silence followed, but it felt companionable rather than uncertain.

Abbie reached into her bag and pulled out a small packet of biscuits.

"I brought these," she said. "In case tea required assistance."

Michael accepted one.

"Prepared," he said.

"Experience," she replied.

They ate in quiet appreciation, crumbs brushed away without fuss.

Michael watched her bracelets slide down her wrist when she reached for her cup. They seemed to be a part of who she was.

"Do you come every day?" Abbie asked.

"Most days," he said. "It helps structure the morning."

She nodded in understanding.

"After my husband Edward died," she said quietly, "mornings were the hardest."

Michael didn't speak immediately.

"Evenings for me, after Janet," he said at last.

Abbie met his eyes.

There was nothing heavy in the exchange. Just recognition.

The market noise rose and fell around them like breathing.

A vendor called out a greeting to Michael as he passed. Michael lifted a hand in return.

"You really do belong here," Abbie said.

Michael shrugged.

"I've had practice belonging to places."

"And people?" she asked lightly.

He thought about that.

"Yes," he said.

Abbie seemed satisfied with the answer.

She finished her tea slowly, watching the market with the relaxed attention of someone who had spent years supervising playgrounds.

Michael realized, not for the first time, that the morning felt shorter than usual.

"I should get on," Abbie said eventually.

Michael nodded.

"Tomorrow?" he asked.

"Tomorrow," she agreed.

She stood, gathering her bag.

"Nice to see you again, Michael Holmes."

"And you, Abbie Payne."

Her bracelets chimed as she walked away.

Michael remained at the table a while longer, finishing his coffee.

When he stood to leave, he noticed something small on the table beside his cup.

A folded paper.

He opened it.

Inside, written in neat, teacherly handwriting, were two words:

Stay warm.

Michael smiled all the way home.

CHAPTER 6

Abbie

Abbie did not intend for the market to become part of her daily routine, yet by the third morning, it already had.

She thought about this as she fastened the clasp of her bracelets and reached automatically for her coat, the motion so familiar it felt borrowed from another life, the rhythm of leaving the house for school before the day had fully begun. It was strange how old habits returned easily when they were good ones.

The air outside was sharper than the day before, carrying the promise of frost that hadn't quite arrived. Abbie tucked her hands into her pockets as she walked, her breath visible in small, steady clouds.

By the time the market came into view, she was already smiling.

Michael sat at their table with a cup in front of him, reading something folded in half, a leaflet or a newspaper page. He looked up as she approached, and the expression that crossed his face was unmistakably recognition.

"Good morning," he said.

"Good morning."

She set her tea down and sat, the chair scraping softly against the stone.

"You're earlier again," he observed.

"So are you," she replied.

That seemed to amuse him.

Abbie wrapped her hands around her cup.

"I used to love Thursdays in the classroom," she said. "They were comfortable days. Not the excitement of Monday or the tiredness of Friday. Just... learning, as well as the anticipation of Friday."

Michael nodded.

"Post offices have steady days too," he said. "Days when nothing urgent happens, but everything important still moves forward."

They sat quietly for a moment, watching the morning assemble itself.

"I found your note," Michael said.

Abbie looked at him over the rim of her cup.

"You did."

"Helpful advice," he added.

She smiled. "I try to be useful."

Michael reached into his coat pocket and placed something on the table between them, a small square of paper, folded once.

Abbie did not open it immediately. She finished her sip of tea first, letting the anticipation sit there like a question she wasn't in a hurry to answer.

Then she unfolded it.

Still time.

The same careful lettering she had noticed before that seemed so familiar. "That's a good one," she said softly.

Michael shrugged, but he looked pleased.

"It seemed appropriate."

"For what?" she asked.

"For mornings," he said.

Abbie folded the paper again and slipped it into her coat pocket.

"I'll keep it," she said.

Michael nodded as if that were the expected outcome.

The market noise swelled around them, and Abbie noticed the folded leaflet Michael had been reading.

"What's that?" she asked.

"Community notice," he said. "Someone retiring from the bakery after forty years."

"That's a long time."

"Yes."

"People build whole lives in places like that," she said.

"They do."

Abbie found herself imagining Michael behind a post office counter, steady, patient, and quietly reassuring. The image fit so well it felt like memory, though she knew it wasn't hers.

Michael, meanwhile, seemed to be studying the movement of the market with particular attention today.

"You like to observe people," she said.

"I always have," he replied.

"Me too."

A comfortable silence followed.

Abbie finished her tea and brushed a stray crumb from the table.

"I think I'll walk along the river today," she said.

"Good idea," Michael replied. "Cold air clears the mind."

"Will you be here tomorrow?"

"Yes."

She nodded, satisfied.

When she stood, her bracelets slid down her wrist with their soft, familiar sound.

"See you tomorrow, Michael."

"See you tomorrow, Abbie."

She walked toward the river path; hands tucked into her coat pockets.

Halfway there, her fingers brushed the folded paper Michael had given her.

She left it there.

Not reading it again.

Not needing to.

Just knowing it was there.

And as she walked beside the slow, steady movement of the Ouse, Abbie realized the market no longer felt like a place she visited.

It felt like somewhere she belonged.

MICHAEL

Michael watched her go, the bracelets at her wrist catching the morning light until she turned the corner and disappeared from view.

He remained seated longer than usual. The market carried on around him with the sound of a crate dropped somewhere nearby, a burst of laughter, and the smell of coffee drifting past.

He lifted his cup, found it empty, and set it down again.

He should have asked to walk with her.

He stood at last, sliding his chair back beneath the table. The folded leaflet went into his coat pocket, followed by the marker he'd used that morning.

Tomorrow, perhaps.

Michael Holmes had spent a lifetime learning that small chances returned if you were patient enough to notice them.

He headed home through the steady rhythm of the market, carrying with him the quiet certainty that the morning routine was no longer only his own.

CHAPTER 7

MICHAEL

The morning carried the faint brightness of a day deciding to be kinder than the last.

Michael noticed it as he crossed the square toward the market, the sunlight touching the upper windows of the buildings before reaching the street. He had brought tea from home today in a travel cup Janet had once bought because it "didn't leak when tipped," a quality she valued more than style.

He arrived at the table before Abbie and sat with both hands around the cup watching the early morning market activity.

"Good morning."

He looked up as Abbie approached their table, her bracelets bright against the gray morning, steam rising from her tea.

"Good morning," he replied.

She sat, settling into the chair as though it had always belonged to her.

"You brought your own today," she said, nodding toward the cup.

"Experimenting," Michael answered.

"Bold."

He chuckled.

They sat quietly for a moment, watching a vendor arrange oranges into a pyramid that immediately leaned to one side.

Abbie sipped her tea.

"Do you cook?" she asked suddenly.

Michael considered.

"Enough to eat," he said. "Janet did most of it."

The name rested between them, simple and unforced.

Abbie did not rush to fill the silence.

"What was she like?" she asked after a moment.

Michael's hands tightened slightly around the cup, not from discomfort, but from the carefulness of memory.

"Kind," he said first. "practical and organized in ways I never managed."

Abbie smiled gently.

"That sounds like a good partnership."

"It was."

He watched the oranges being rearranged.

"She liked routines," he continued. "We always had tea at four. Even on holidays. Especially on holidays."

Abbie laughed softly.

"That sounds familiar."

Michael nodded.

"She could make a room feel settled just by being in it."

The words surprised him as he said them. They felt accurate in a way memory sometimes resisted.

Abbie didn't respond immediately, which Michael appreciated.

"Edward was like that in the garden," she said after a moment. "Things grew better when he was near them."

Michael nodded again.

"She was ill for a while," Michael said, his voice steady. "Janet."

Abbie's eyes softened, but she did not interrupt.

"I cared for her at home," he continued. "It felt... important."

He paused, searching for the right word.

"Complete," he said at last.

Abbie's hand rested lightly on the table between them, not reaching across, just present.

"Yes," she said.

They sat together in the quiet that followed until a dog barked nearby, startling them both slightly. Abbie laughed first, and Michael followed.

"Life continues," she said.

"It does."

Michael realized the memory did not ache the way it once had. Speaking Janet's name felt like opening a window rather than reopening a wound.

He reached into his pocket and pulled out a small, folded paper.

"Something for you," he said.

Abbie opened it carefully.

You're doing fine.

Her eyes lifted to his.

"That's a teacher message," she said.

"Borrowed wisdom," Michael replied.

Abbie folded the paper and slipped it into the small side pocket of her bag.

"I'll keep it," she said.

Michael nodded, satisfied.

They finished their drinks slowly, watching the market fill with people.

When Abbie stood to leave, she paused.

"I'm glad you told me about Janet," she said.

"So am I."

She walked away, bracelets chiming softly.

Michael remained seated, watching the sunlight finally reach the tabletop.

He remembered Janet laughing in their kitchen, sunlight catching the steam from a kettle.

He remembered the quiet after.

Both memories felt steady now.

After a moment, he stood and gathered his cup.

As he left the market, he found himself thinking that Janet would have liked Abbie, and that, he realized, felt like another kind of beginning.

ABBIE

Abbie arrived at the market with the faintest scent of soil still on her hands.

She had been in the garden longer than she intended, loosening the earth around the stubborn lavender plant Edward had insisted would survive anything. It had not, not yet, but Abbie continued to try.

Edward would have approved of persistence.

Michael was already at the table when she approached, his hands wrapped around his cup in the now-familiar way.

"Good morning," she said.

"Good morning, Abbie."

She sat, setting her tea beside his cup. The market felt warmer today, though the air was just as cold.

"I was in the garden," she explained, brushing her palms together. "Fighting with lavender."

Michael nodded solemnly.

"Lavender can be stubborn."

"You sound experienced."

"Janet liked herbs," he said. "We had rosemary that refused to die."

Abbie smiled.

"That sounds right."

They watched a pair of vendors struggle with a tangled length of rope.

"Edward loved gardening," Abbie said after a moment.

The name came easily.

Michael listened.

"He believed plants were patient teachers," she continued. "He said you could learn everything important from watching something grow slowly."

Michael considered this.

"That sounds wise."

"It was," she said.

She wrapped her hands around her tea.

"He grew tomatoes that never tasted the same when I tried," she added, smiling at the memory. "I followed his instructions exactly. Still not the same."

Michael chuckled.

"Some things don't transfer and I am just not good with plants."

"Not everyone is."

"He was ill for a short time," Abbie said. "Not long, but long enough to say goodbye."

Michael nodded.

They did not look at each other immediately.

"I still talk to him in the garden sometimes," she added, almost casually.

"That makes sense. Sometimes I talk to Janet, especially when I can't find something. She had a way of remembering where I possibly might have put things." Michael said.

Abbie laughed, hesitated, and reached into her bag.

"I brought something," she said.

She slid a small, folded card across the table.

Michael opened it.

Inside, written in careful teacher's script:

You're not alone.

Michael looked up and Abbie smiled.

"Borrowed wisdom," she said.

Michael nodded once, folding the card and placing it carefully in his pocket.

They finished their drinks slowly, watching the morning continue around them.

Abbie noticed something then, that there was a familiarity between them now.

Edward would have liked Michael, she thought.

The realization surprised her, but it did not hurt.

It felt like permission.

When she stood to leave, the lavender scent rose faintly from her sleeves.

"Tomorrow," she said.

"Tomorrow," Michael replied.

As she walked away, Abbie found herself thinking that the garden might finally be ready for spring, even if winter had not quite finished yet.

Abbie hesitated at the edge of the market before turning toward the river.

The morning had been brighter than expected, sunlight sparkling along the water, and the towpath looked almost inviting.

She adjusted the strap of her bag and began walking.

Behind her, she heard someone call her name and she paused, glancing behind her.

Michael caught up with her. "Are you heading along the river?"

"Yes," she replied. "Just for a bit."

There was the smallest beat of silence.

Then:

"May I join you?"

Abbie smiled.

"I'd like that."

They walked side by side at first without speaking, the rhythm of their steps settling into something easy. The river moved steadily beside them, boats shifting gently in their moorings.

"It's quieter here," Abbie said.

"Yes."

They passed a narrowboat with a small dog perched watchfully at the stern. Conversation came in small pieces, her teaching memories, his post office ones, and how they spent their days.

The path narrowed slightly ahead.

Abbie turned her head to say something—and heard the sudden rush of wheels behind them.

"Mind—!"

The cyclist came fast around the bend, looking over his shoulder instead of ahead.

Michael reacted without thinking.

His hand closed around Abbie's arm, pulling her sharply toward him just as the bicycle shot past, close enough for the wind of it to brush her coat.

The moment passed in a blur.

Silence followed.

Abbie realized she was standing very close to Michael.

His hand still rested at her elbow, his body shielding her.

Her other hand had caught at his coat without meaning to.

They both remained still for a heartbeat longer than necessary.

"Are you alright?" he asked quietly.

"Yes."

He loosened his grip, but not entirely.

"I should have..." he began.

"No," she said gently. "You were paying attention."

He released her then, stepping back half a pace.

Abbie's pulse took a few minutes to settle.

She became suddenly aware of how solid he had felt when he pulled her toward him. How natural it had been to lean into that steadiness and how suddenly she wished he hadn't released her.

Michael cleared his throat softly.

"Cyclists," he said.

"Yes."

They resumed walking, though closer now.

After a while, Abbie said, "Thank you."

"You're welcome."

He hesitated.

"I didn't think," he said.

"I know."

That, somehow, felt important.

They walked for nearly an hour before turning back toward the market.

When they reached the square, they paused where the path met the stones.

"Well," Abbie said lightly, "that was an adventure."

"Indeed."

She adjusted her bracelets, though they had not shifted.

"I'm glad you came."

"So am I."

They parted with their usual "Tomorrow," but something in the word felt different now.

Later that afternoon, as Abbie stood in her kitchen rinsing a teacup, she found herself remembering the brief, steady warmth of his arm around her.

It had not felt startling.

It had felt... right.

Across town, Michael sat at his small desk, staring at a blank scrap of paper before writing two words carefully in block letters:

Pay attention.

He folded the note and slipped it into his coat pocket.

Just in case.

CHAPTER 9

MICHAEL

The rain began before Michael reached the market.

Not a heavy rain, just the fine, persistent kind that settled into the air as if it had always been there. The stone underfoot darkened, and the canvas awnings above the stalls sagged slightly with collected water.

Michael pulled his collar higher and kept walking.

He wondered briefly whether Abbie would come in weather like this.

He found himself hoping she would.

The shared tables were mostly empty when he arrived. He chose the one nearest the covered edge of the market, where the awning extended far enough to keep the chairs dry.

He sat, set his cup down, and listened to the soft patter of rain on canvas.

He noticed the towpath from where he sat.

He hadn't meant to think about it again.

But he did.

The rush of wheels.

The feel of her arm beneath his hand.

The brief moment when she had leaned into him without hesitation and how he wanted to feel that again.

He adjusted the position of his cup, then adjusted it again.

The market sounded different in rain, quieter and closer, as if the weather drew people inward.

"Good morning."

Michael looked up quickly.

Abbie stood there, hair slightly damp, bracelets hidden beneath her coat sleeve as she shook the rain off her umbrella before closing it.

"Good morning," he said, relief arriving before he could stop it.

"You found the dry table," she said, sitting down.

"Experience," he replied.

She laughed softly and blew across her tea.

"I almost didn't come," she admitted.

"I'm glad you did."

The words slipped out simply, without hesitation.

Abbie's smile warmed. "Me too."

They sat listening to the rain for a moment.

"Did you sleep well?" she asked.

"Yes."

A small pause.

"And you?"

"Yes."

Michael cleared his throat.

"I've been thinking about yesterday."

Abbie's bracelets chimed softly as she folded her hands on the table.

"So have I."

He nodded once.

"I should have been walking on the outside," he said.

She looked at him, surprised. "That isn't what I was thinking."

"No?"

"No." She hesitated only a moment before continuing. "I was thinking that I felt very safe."

The words settled between them.

Michael did not answer immediately.

The market remained quiet around them, vendors still setting up.

"I'm glad," he said at last.

Abbie met his eyes. "So am I."

A breeze moved across the square, lifting the edge of her scarf.

Michael resisted the instinct to reach out and straighten it.

Instead, he picked up his cup and Abbie reached for hers at the same time.

Their fingers touched, but neither pulled away. The contact lasted just long enough to be felt, and not long enough to be remarked upon.

Abbie smiled, faint but certain.

"You don't have to walk on the outside," she said.

Michael looked at her. "I might anyway."

She laughed softly.

They drank their tea.

Conversation resumed, but something had shifted, an awareness that something had changed between them yesterday.

Michael found their quiet conversation companionable in a deeper way than before.

"Rain changes everything," Abbie said.

"It slows things down."

"I don't mind that," she replied.

"Neither do I."

A longer silence followed, comfortable and shared.

Michael watched the steam from their cups curl upward and disappear into the cool air.

"You said evenings were hardest," Abbie said gently.

Michael nodded.

"They were quieter," he said. "After Janet died."

Abbie listened without looking away.

"I didn't know what to do with them," he continued. "Mornings had tasks. Evenings had... memory."

Abbie's hands tightened slightly around her cup.

"Mornings were hardest for me," she said. "The house felt wrong without Edward making noise."

Michael nodded.

Rain tapped steadily above them.

"I think," Abbie said after a moment, "we learn new shapes for time."

Michael considered that.

"Yes," he said. "We do."

They watched a puddle form at the edge of the stones.

"Life afterwards changes," Michael added.

"It does," Abbie agreed.

The market carried on around them, softened by the rain.

Michael reached into his pocket and pulled out a folded scrap of paper, placing it between them.

Abbie opened it.

Stay anyway.

She smiled. "That's a good one."

"It's a rainy-day message," he said.

Abbie slipped the paper into her coat pocket.

"I brought something too," she said.

She handed him a small square of paper torn from a notebook.

Michael opened it.

You're doing better than you think.

He nodded slowly.

Michael realized something. The morning no longer felt like time he was filling but felt like time he was sharing.

When Abbie stood to leave, she did not step away immediately.

"I'm glad you asked to join me yesterday," she said.

"So am I."

She hesitated, then added:

"I enjoyed your company."

Michael felt that land more deeply than he expected.

"I'd like to do it again." he said. "Tomorrow I'll get our coffee and tea...okay?"

Abbie nodded in agreement. "Tomorrow."

As she walked away, Michael realized the word tomorrow no longer meant routine.

It meant intention.

He remained seated, listening to the last drops fall from the awning.

He thought, not for the first time, that small routines could become important without asking permission.

And that perhaps, without noticing when it happened, the market table had become less about coffee...and more about companionship.

CHAPTER 10

ABBIE

The market smelled faintly of cinnamon that morning. Abbie followed the scent past the bakery stall before reaching the table, where Michael already sat with two cups in front of him.

"I took a risk," he said as she approached.

Abbie raised an eyebrow.

"One tea," he added, sliding the second cup toward her.

She lifted it, amused.

"Milk, no sugar," she said.

"I hoped so."

"You hoped correctly."

She sat, warming her hands around the cup. The gesture felt so natural now that she didn't notice herself doing it until after she had already settled.

"You're getting used to this," she said.

Michael smiled. "Routine helps."

They drank quietly for a moment while the market moved into its morning rhythm.

A vendor across the way chalked prices onto a small board, the chalk squeaking faintly with each number.

Abbie watched Michael reach for something in his coat pocket.

A marker.

He uncapped it and pulled a scrap of paper toward him, writing something slowly and carefully, as he often did.

Abbie found herself watching his hand.

The letters formed in neat block printing that was deliberate, steady, and evenly spaced.

A small ripple of recognition passed through her. Not memory exactly, but more like the feeling of knowing a song before remembering where you'd heard it.

Michael finished writing and folded the paper once before sliding it toward her.

Abbie opened it.

Sunshine today.

She smiled.

"That's optimistic," she said.

Michael glanced toward the pale sky. "Hopeful."

Abbie folded the note, but her attention lingered on the shape of the letters.

Something about them felt... familiar.

She studied his hand as he recapped the marker and tucked it behind his ear.

"I used to know someone who wrote like that," she said.

Michael looked up.

"Like what?"

"Careful," she said. "As if the words mattered."

Michael considered this.

"They usually do," he replied.

Abbie nodded, though her attention drifted somewhere else, to a classroom long ago, shared textbooks, penciled notes in margins that had made her laugh when she should have been studying.

The memory refused to sharpen; it was hazy and she couldn't quite grasp it.

A child dropped a coin nearby, and the small clatter broke her concentration.

She blinked and returned to the present.

"Do you think," she said, "that handwriting stays the same even when everything else changes?"

Michael thought about that.

"I suppose it might," he said.

The market noise swelled around them again.

Abbie took another sip of tea, letting the warmth settle.

She didn't mention the strange familiarity again.

Some thoughts needed time.

When she stood to leave, Michael handed her another folded paper without comment.

She slipped it into her bag without opening it.

"I'll read it later," she said.

Michael nodded.

"Tomorrow?"

She smiled. "Tomorrow."

Abbie remembered the note when she emptied her bag onto the kitchen table. It slipped free from between her book and her gloves, landing lightly beside the sugar bowl. She had almost forgotten it.

The house was quiet in the way she had come to expect, and afternoon light stretched across the table, catching the edge of the folded paper.

She washed her cup, first, and then she returned to the

table and opened the note. Michael's careful lettering filled the small square of paper:

Some things return slowly.

Abbie stood still for a moment.

The words settled into her chest like warmth spreading through cold hands.

The note felt less like a message and more like reassurance, the kind she used to give students when understanding took longer than they wanted it to.

She folded the paper again, more carefully this time, and slipped it into the small drawer beside the kettle.

A place for things worth keeping.

Then she turned back to the window, where the garden waited in its winter stillness, and found herself thinking about block letters in pencil, encouragement written beside mistakes, and the slow return of memories that had never truly disappeared.

"Slowly," she said aloud.

CHAPTER 11

MICHAEL

Michael brought his markers with him on purpose that morning. They rested in his coat pocket as he crossed the square toward the market, tapping lightly against one another with each step. The sound reminded him of sorting stamps into neat rows behind the post office counter, small, orderly preparations for something that hadn't happened yet.

The rain from the previous morning had washed the stones clean, leaving the market brighter than usual.

Abbie arrived a few minutes after he sat down.

"Good morning," she said.

"Good morning."

She set her tea beside his coffee and settled into the chair across from him with an ease that no longer felt new.

"You look prepared," she said, nodding toward the markers he'd placed on the table.

Michael glanced at them.

"So it seems."

Abbie smiled.

"Planning to start a lesson?"

"Possibly."

The market hummed around them, a low, steady sound that felt like breathing.

Michael turned one of the paper cups slowly in his hands.

Without thinking too much about it, he uncapped the black marker and wrote across the side of the cup in careful block letters:

Courage.

The word came easily.

He set the marker down and slid the cup toward Abbie.

She looked at the word and went still.

Not frozen, just quiet in a way that felt different from their usual silences.

Michael waited.

Abbie traced the edge of the lettering with her eyes.

"My goodness," she said softly.

Michael tilted his head.

"What?"

"That word," she said. "Someone used to write that in the margins of my math worksheets."

Michael felt something shift in his chest. *Could it be that she remembers?*

"Oh?"

She nodded slowly.

"I was terrible at fractions," she said, smiling faintly. "Someone would write *Courage* beside the problems I got wrong."

Michael looked down at the marker in his hand.

"I remember fractions," he said, his cheeks flushing a little.

Abbie's gaze sharpened slightly. "Strange thing to remember."

"Not really," Michael replied.

She lifted the cup and took a sip.

Michael watched the memory move behind her eyes, not fully formed yet, but closer than before.

He folded a small piece of paper from his pocket and slid it across the table.

Abbie opened it.

Nearly there.

She looked up at him.

"That sounds mysterious."

"Patience," he said.

Abbie laughed.

"I used to say that to children who wanted to skip ahead in books."

"Wise advice."

She shook her head, amused.

"You're enjoying this."

"Perhaps."

The market filled with sunlight, bouncing off the wet stones.

Abbie finished her tea slowly, still glancing now and then at the word on the cup.

Michael sensed the recognition building, like a letter nearing its destination, not yet delivered, but close.

When Abbie stood to leave, she hesitated.

"I'm going to think about that word," she said.

Michael nodded.

"Good."

She picked up the cup carefully and carried it with her as she walked away.

Michael remained seated, watching the market move around him.

He remembered a classroom desk, a shared pencil, a girl who laughed easily when she made mistakes.

He hadn't thought about that in years, but several days ago, he had remembered.

He capped the marker and slipped it back into his pocket.

Soon, he thought, soon he hoped she would remember.

And somehow, the waiting felt as important as the knowing.

CHAPTER 12

Abbie

Abbie woke with the word still in her mind.
Courage.

It lingered there as she dressed, as she fastened her bracelets, as she poured hot water over the teabag in her mug. The memory it tugged at remained just beyond reach, like a name she almost remembered.

Some things return slowly.

Michael's note had been right.

She carried the thought with her all the way to the market.

Michael was already seated when she arrived, sunlight catching the edge of the table between them. He looked up as she approached, his expression settling into its now-familiar warmth.

"Good morning," he said.

"Good morning."

She sat, setting her tea down with more care than usual.

"I remembered something," she said.

Michael nodded once, as if he had been expecting this.

"I thought you might."

Abbie studied his face for a moment, the calm eyes, the patient stillness.

"Did you go to St. Bartholomew's School?" she asked.

Michael's smile deepened, just slightly.

"Yes," he said.

The market noise seemed to soften around them.

Abbie let out a small breath she hadn't realized she was holding.

"Oh," she said. "Oh, my goodness."

Michael waited.

"You sat next to me in mathematics," she said slowly. "Second row from the windows."

Michael chuckled softly.

"That sounds right."

"You used to write in the margins of my math worksheets when I got stuck," she continued, the memory assembling itself piece by piece.

Michael looked down at the table.

"I hoped you didn't mind."

"I didn't," she said. "Your words always made me feel better."

He lifted his eyes again.

"Well," he said, "that's what I wanted them to do."

Abbie laughed and shook her head, "Michael Holmes. Of course."

The name slid right into place in her memories.

"You always finished your work early," she added. "Then pretended to still be working."

Michael smiled.

"I wasn't very convincing."

"No," she agreed.

Courage.

Try again.

Nearly there.

Abbie felt warmth spread through her chest.

"I remember your handwriting," she said. "That's what it was."

Michael nodded.

"I remembered your laugh and that you always had extra biscuits you shared with me." he said.

She blinked.

"You remember that?"

"Yes."

The simplicity of the answer made her throat tighten unexpectedly.

"I can't believe we never really talked outside of that class," she said.

"We were shy," Michael replied.

"That sounds like me," she said.

"And me."

They sat quietly, letting the shared past settle between them.

Not overwhelming.

Not sad.

Just... found.

A vendor walked past carrying a stack of wooden crates dropped one, breaking the stillness.

Abbie picked up her tea again, smiling.

"Well," she said, "this explains a great deal."

Michael tilted his head.

"Does it?"

"Yes," she replied. "It explains why you're so patient with fractions."

Michael laughed.

"And why you bring biscuits," he said.

Abbie shook her head, amused.

"Imagine that," she said. "All these years."

Michael looked around the market at the stalls and the people. The ordinary morning continuing as if nothing remarkable had happened, yet everything felt slightly different.

"Funny where life brings you back to," he said.

Abbie nodded.

"Yes," she said softly. "It is."

She reached into her bag and pulled out a folded piece of paper, sliding it across the table.

Michael opened it.

Found you.

He looked up, smiling.

They sat there together, the market moving around them, the past no longer distant but gently returned.

And for the first time since they had met again at the table, the familiarity between them felt complete, no longer a question waiting to be answered, but a memory redis-covered.

"Tomorrow?" Abbie said.

"Tomorrow," Michael replied.

And now, the word carried history with it.

CHAPTER 13

MICHAEL

Michael arrived at the market and Abbie appeared a moment later, slowing when she saw him already at their table.

"You're ahead of me today," she said.

"Practice," Michael replied.

As they sat, she took a sip of her tea and looked over at him with a small smile that felt different now, more familiar, and less tentative.

"Do you remember Mr. Wilkes?" Abbie asked.

"The mathematics teacher?"

"Yes."

Michael nodded.

"He always wore the same brown jacket."

"And said 'steady now' whenever anyone panicked," Abbie added.

Michael chuckled. "He said that a lot."

"I needed it often," she said.

"You did fine," Michael replied automatically.

Abbie smiled at the familiarity of the reassurance.

"You always said that," she said.

Michael hadn't realized.

They sat quietly, letting the memory sit between them like an old photograph.

"I remember you lending people pencils," Abbie said. "You always had extras."

Michael shrugged.

"My father believed in preparedness."

"Well, it saved me many times."

A vendor called out a greeting to Michael as he passed. Michael returned the wave, then turned back to Abbie.

"I remember you reading during lunch," he said.

Abbie looked surprised.

"I did?"

"Yes. By the windows."

She laughed softly.

"I'd forgotten that."

"You read quickly."

"Only stories," she said. "Never fractions."

Michael smiled.

Abbie turned her cup slowly in her hands.

"Life is strange," she said. "All those years between then and now."

Michael nodded.

"Full years," he said.

"Yes."

Neither of them listed what those years contained.

They didn't need to.

After a moment, Michael reached into his pocket and slid a folded note across the table.

Abbie opened it.

Always did.

She looked up, puzzled.

"You always did fine," he said.

Abbie's expression softened.

"Well," she said, folding the note carefully, "thank you for continuing the lesson."

Michael smiled.

Abbie reached into her bag.

"I have something too," she said.

She handed him a small square of paper.

Michael opened it.

Still here.

He nodded once.

The words felt larger than they appeared.

They finished their drinks slowly, watching the market fill with people who did not know the small history sitting at the table between them.

They stood beside the table longer than usual.

The market had thinned slightly, the late-morning quiet settling in.

Abbie folded her note—*Always did*—and tucked it into her bag with care.

Michael remained where he was.

"I'm glad we remembered," she said.

"So am I."

The words lingered between them.

Abbie hesitated, then stepped closer, not abruptly, not theatrically, just enough that the space between them narrowed in a way it had not before.

"Michael," she said softly, "you were very kind to me back then."

He shook his head lightly.

"I only wrote what was true."

She studied him for a moment, the familiar set of his

shoulders, the careful steadiness that had once sat next to her in a classroom.

Without overthinking it, she reached out and touched his arm.

"Thank you," she said again.

The contact felt deliberate and neither moved for a heartbeat.

Then Abbie did something neither of them had expected.

She stepped forward and folded her arms around him.

Michael stiffened for half a second, surprised, and then returned the embrace with equal steadiness, his hands resting carefully at her back.

She felt smaller than he remembered.

The market continued around them as if nothing had changed.

But something had.

CHAPTER 14

bbie stepped back first.

The hug had come without warning, one moment she had been laughing in disbelief, the next her arms were around him.

Now she felt suddenly aware of it.

"Sorry," she said quickly, though she wasn't entirely sure she meant it.

Michael looked as surprised as she felt.

"I don't mind," he said.

That didn't help her composure nearly as much as she hoped.

She picked up her bag from the chair.

"I should probably—"

"Have lunch with me."

The words came out before Michael appeared to fully consider them.

They both paused.

Then he added, slightly more carefully, "If you're not in a hurry."

Abbie tilted her head, studying him.

The shy boy she remembered from school would never have said something like that so directly.

But the gentleness in his voice was the same.

"I'm not," she said.

They walked out of the market together.

York was alive with the steady rhythm of late morning, the distant bells from the Minster marking the hour.

They turned instinctively toward the narrow streets leading to the Shambles.

For a few minutes they walked without speaking.

Not awkwardly.

Just... absorbing.

Abbie found herself glancing at him more than once.

He had grown older, of course. His hair thinner at the temples, his posture slightly more deliberate.

But the quiet steadiness she remembered had not changed.

If anything, it had deepened.

"Did you ever imagine," she said finally, "that we'd meet again like this?"

"No," he said.

She smiled faintly.

"Neither did I."

They reached a small stall where the scent of roasted meat drifted warmly into the street.

"Yorkshire pudding wrap?" Michael asked.

"That sounds dangerously good."

He ordered two.

They found a bench along the edge of the street where people passed slowly between the shops.

Abbie took a bite and laughed softly.

"Oh, that's excellent."

Michael seemed pleased by her approval.

"You always did like food," he said.

"I did?"

"You were very enthusiastic about the school lunches."

She laughed again.

"I had completely forgotten that."

He watched her for a moment.

She noticed it, though she pretended not to.

It had been many years since anyone had looked at her with that kind of quiet attention.

"Did you know?" he asked.

"Know what?"

"That I wrote those notes."

She hesitated.

"Yes. Well, I suspected, but I didn't think you wanted me to know, so I acted like I didn't."

That surprised him.

"You did?"

"Not at the beginning," she said thoughtfully. "but then one day I saw you do it when I wasn't looking."

He looked down at his wrap.

"I was not very brave then."

"You were kinder than you realized."

The words slipped out before she could consider them.

They sat quietly for a moment after that.

People moved around them, voices blending into the warm hum of the street.

Abbie found herself studying the small details she hadn't noticed earlier, the steadiness of his hands and the way he listened fully when she spoke.

She wondered what the years between then and now had been like for him.

And whether he was wondering the same about her.

When they finished eating, Michael crumpled the paper neatly.

"Walk a little more?" he asked.

"Yes."

They moved slowly through the narrow street, sunlight catching the crooked beams of the old buildings.

It felt strangely easy, yet familiar and new at the same time.

Abbie realized, with a small flicker of surprise, that she didn't want the afternoon to end yet.

"Well," she said lightly, her voice slightly softer than usual.

"Well," he replied.

They both smiled, the air between them felt altered, charged not with excitement but with certainty.

"I'm glad we remembered," she said.

"So am I."

They turned out of the narrow street and toward a quieter lane.

The pavement dipped unevenly where the stones met the road.

Abbie stepped down without paying much attention.

Michael reached out automatically.

His hand closed gently around her elbow.

"Careful."

The word was quiet but instinctive.

She steadied herself, surprised more by the contact than the curb.

"Oh," she said lightly. "Thank you."

He released her immediately.

Perhaps too quickly.

But the brief warmth of his hand lingered longer than either of them expected.

They continued walking.

Abbie kept her eyes on the path ahead, though she was suddenly aware of him in a way she hadn't been moments before.

MICHAEL

Michael, for his part, pretended to study a shop window they passed.

He had not meant to touch her.

At least, that was what he told himself.

Still, he found himself quietly pleased that she did not move away.

Michael watched her laugh at something passing in the street and felt an odd, familiar pull of memory.

For a moment he had the faint impression that he had once spent a great deal of time simply watching her like this, quietly, from across a room, and saying very little. The thought slipped away before he could examine it.

Later, when they reached the corner where their paths would separate, Abbie paused.

"This was a very good lunch invitation," she said.

"I'm glad you accepted."

She smiled, that same thoughtful smile he remembered from years ago.

"Well," she said, adjusting the bracelets at her wrist, "it would have been rude not to."

She turned to go, then looked back briefly.

"See you tomorrow morning?"

"Yes," he said.

After she disappeared into the flow of people, he remained standing there for a moment longer. He realized that the memory of the classroom no longer felt distant or separate from the present. It felt like a letter delayed in the post but finally delivered.

He turned toward home, thinking that sometimes the smallest moments, a forgotten memory, and how a morning that began like any other could end with the quiet feeling that something new had begun.

CHAPTER 15

ABBIE

Abbie set her bag on the kitchen table and stood there for a moment, listening to the familiar stillness.

She removed her bracelets one by one, placing them beside the sink.

She could still feel the warm steadiness of the hug and the way his hands had rested against her back. She had not been held like that in years, not since Edward.

She walked into the sitting room and paused beside the photograph on the mantel. Edward's smile looked the same as it always had, kind and familiar.

"I haven't forgotten you," she said quietly.

She touched the frame lightly.

"But I am still here."

The sentence surprised her.

She sank into the chair by the window and let the memory of the morning return, Michael's expression when he had said her name, and how good it felt standing close to him.

She exhaled slowly.

"I think," she said softly to the empty room, "I'm allowed."

The permission did not arrive with tears, but a sense of relief.

She leaned back in her chair and allowed herself, for the first time without resistance, to imagine walking beside Michael again, not as a memory of school days, not as companionship, but as something new and chosen.

And when she rose to turn out the lights, she knew that tomorrow would no longer be simply habit.

It would be possibility.

MICHAEL

Michael sat at his small desk long after the light outside had faded.

He had intended to sort through old papers, an envelope here, a receipt there, but the pen in his hand had not moved in several minutes.

He could still feel the weight of her in his arms. He leaned back in the chair and closed his eyes briefly. He had not expected how natural it would feel, or how long the feel of her would stay with him.

The memory shifted further back, uninvited but clear, a narrow classroom at St. Bartholomew's, wooden desks arranged in rows, sunlight catching dust in the air.

Abbie in the seat next to him, laughing when she missed a fraction, brushing hair behind her ear when she concentrated.

He had been thirteen and painfully unsure of himself.

He had known many things then, fractions, train schedules, and the exact way to organize his stamp collection, but he had not known how to speak to a girl who made his chest feel tight simply by turning towards him.

So he had done what he knew.

He had written in the margins of her math papers when they exchanged them to correct as the teacher gave the answers.

Try again.

Nearly there.

Courage.

He had written encouragement because it was safer than confession, safer than risking embarrassment, safer than risking being seen, and in doing so, she had never known.

He opened his eyes and stared at the blank sheet of paper in front of him.

"I should have said something," he murmured.

But even as he said it, he understood that he could not have.

The boy he had been had not known how.

He had loved her quietly.

The hug that morning had not felt new.

It had felt like something long delayed.

Michael stood and walked to the window.

The town lights shimmered faintly in the distance.

He thought of Janet, of the years they had shared, steady and real. He did not regret them. Not for a moment.

But what he felt now did not erase what had been.

It simply acknowledged what had once been unfinished.

He exhaled slowly.

"I won't do that again," he said softly into the quiet room.

This time, he would not hide; this time, he would speak.

He returned to the desk and wrote two words in careful block letters on the page before him.

Be brave.

He folded the paper and placed it inside his coat pocket.

Not for her.

For himself.

And for the first time since he had been thirteen, the idea of telling her how he felt did not seem impossible.

It seemed... possible.

CHAPTER 16

ABBIE

The market was busy enough that morning to make conversation pause and resume in small intervals.

Abbie didn't mind. The movement around them felt lively, a reminder that the world rarely stood still long enough for anyone to notice their own thoughts too closely.

Michael handed her tea without asking.

"Thank you," she said.

"You're welcome."

They watched a nearby vendor struggle to balance a stack of paper cups on a narrow shelf inside a small coffee stall. The stack tipped, he caught it, and then it tipped again.

Abbie smiled.

"That looks familiar," she said.

Michael followed her gaze.

"Difficult geometry," he replied.

"Very."

They sat for a moment longer, observing the quiet

choreography of the stall, pouring, handing cups across a counter, wiping spills, and greeting customers.

Abbie found herself leaning forward slightly.

"I always liked school fairs," she said. "Serving tea to parents, pretending we were running proper cafés."

Michael nodded.

"I helped at a charity table once," he said. "Sold bars of chocolate for fundraising."

"Did you enjoy it?"

"Yes."

Abbie watched a woman accept a cup from the stall vendor and walk away smiling.

"It looks pleasant," she said.

"It does."

The thought came to her easily then, as many of her best ideas once had, not fully formed, just curious.

"We could do that," she said.

Michael looked at her.

"Sell chocolate?" he asked.

Abbie laughed.

"No. Coffee and tea."

Michael's expression remained thoughtful, not dismissive.

"I've often imagined doing just that. Could we?" he said.

Abbie shrugged lightly.

"Perhaps not. But it would be nice."

She sipped her tea.

"Seeing people start their mornings," she added. "Offering something warm."

Michael glanced again at the stall, then back at Abbie.

"Yes," he said. "It would."

The idea hovered between them.

A breeze carried the smell of roasted beans across the square and

Abbie reached into her bag, pulled out a small piece of paper, wrote on it, folded it, and handed it to him.

Michael opened it.

Why not?

He smiled.

"That sounds like a teacher encouraging risk," he said.

"Exactly."

Michael took a moment before reaching into his own pocket for paper and pen. After a minute, he slid a note toward her.

Abbie unfolded it.

Maybe.

She laughed softly.

"That's a postmaster's version of courage."

"Measured optimism," he replied.

They sat quietly, both glancing now and then at the coffee stall across the market.

Abbie didn't mention the thought again.

She didn't need to.

Ideas, like memories, often returned when they were ready.

When she stood to leave, she felt lighter than she had in years, not because anything had changed, but because something might.

"Tomorrow," she said.

"Tomorrow."

As Abbie walked home, she found herself imagining a small wooden stall, a window opening onto the market, cups lined neatly in rows.

And words written carefully along their sides.

The image stayed with her all the way home.

CHAPTER 17

MICHAEL

Michael noticed the coffee stall before Abbie arrived. The vendor was alone that morning, moving quickly between the kettle, the cups, and the small tin holding coins. A line had formed, not long, but steady enough to keep the man from pausing.

Michael watched for a moment, remembering the comfortable busyness of the post office counter, hands moving without needing thought, conversation flowing in small pieces between transactions.

"Good morning."

Abbie set her tea down beside him.

"Good morning," he replied, nodding toward the stall. "Busy today."

She followed his gaze.

"Oh dear," she said. "He looks overwhelmed."

The vendor fumbled with a stack of lids, dropping two to the ground.

Abbie stood without hesitation.

Michael watched her walk to the stall, bracelets bright against her sleeve. She spoke briefly to the vendor, who nodded with visible relief.

Abbie began handing cups across the counter.

Michael stood a moment later and joined them.

"What can I do?" he asked.

The vendor handed him a cloth.

"Wipe and stack," he said gratefully.

Michael nodded.

The work felt immediately familiar, small motions repeated with purpose. He wiped the counter, stacked cups, arranged lids into neat rows.

Abbie greeted customers with the calm cheerfulness of someone who had managed classrooms full of restless children.

"Milk?"

"Sugar?"

"Careful, it's hot."

Michael found himself smiling.

For half an hour, the three of them worked together in an easy rhythm.

The line shortened, the kettle quieted, and at last, the vendor leaned against the side of the stall and exhaled.

"Thank you," he said. "That happens sometimes when the morning rush surprises me."

"Happy to help," Abbie replied.

Michael nodded.

The vendor poured two fresh drinks and handed them across the counter.

"On the house."

They accepted.

Back at the table, Abbie laughed softly.

"Well," she said, "that was fun."

Michael agreed.

"Yes."

They sipped their drinks, watching the stall continue at a calmer pace.

Abbie turned her cup slowly in her hands.

"It felt natural," she said.

"It did…and comfortable."

Michael considered the feeling carefully.

The same comfort he had known behind the post office counter when people stepped forward with letters and questions and stories they didn't always realize they were telling.

Abbie reached into her bag and slid a folded note across the table.

Michael opened it.

See?

He smiled.

"Yes," he said.

He reached into his pocket and wrote quickly on a scrap of paper.

He slid it back to her.

Abbie unfolded it.

Possible.

She nodded, pleased.

The market continued its steady rhythm around them.

Michael realized something then. Helping at the stall had not felt like trying something new; it had felt like remembering something he already knew how to do.

He finished his drink slowly.

When Abbie stood to leave, she paused.

"We could help again tomorrow," she said.

Michael nodded. "I'd like that."

As she walked away, Michael remained seated, watching the small coffee stall across the market.

The idea no longer felt like imagination but felt like the beginning of a plan.

CHAPTER 18

Abbie

Abbie arrived at the market with a small notebook in her bag.

She hadn't planned to bring it.

It had simply found its way into her hands that morning, the way school supplies once did when she sensed a lesson forming.

Michael was already seated.

"Good morning," he said.

"Good morning."

They both looked toward the coffee stall.

The vendor waved when he saw them.

"Busy again?" Abbie asked.

Michael shook his head. "Quiet today."

They sat, sipping their drinks, watching customers drift in and out of the square.

After a moment, Abbie reached into her bag and placed the notebook on the table.

Michael raised an eyebrow.

"Planning something?"

"Thinking," she said.

She opened the notebook to a blank page.

The paper felt strangely familiar beneath her hand.

"What would we need?" she asked.

Michael did not pretend to misunderstand.

"A kettle," he said.

She wrote it down.

"Cups," he added.

She nodded, writing again.

"Table," she said.

"Shelter."

"Milk."

"Tea."

"Coffee."

The list grew.

Neither of them rushed.

Abbie paused.

"Permission," she said.

Michael nodded.

"Yes."

She wrote the word carefully.

"And time," he added.

She smiled.

"That we have."

They looked at the list together.

It wasn't long or complicated.

Abbie closed the notebook.

"Well," she said.

Michael waited.

"I think we could do this," she said.

Michael looked toward the coffee stall again, the small wooden structure, the handwritten price board, and the steady exchange of cups and coins.

"Yes," he said.

The certainty in his voice surprised them both.

Abbie laughed softly.

"That sounded like a decision."

"It did."

They sat quietly, letting the idea settle.

Abbie reached into her bag and after a minute with a pen and piece of paper, she slid a folded note across the table.

Michael opened it.

Let's.

He nodded once.

Michael picked up a marker and wrote on a scrap of paper.

He handed it to her.

Abbie opened it.

Together.

She folded the paper carefully and slipped it into the notebook.

The market bells from a nearby church tower rang the hour.

Neither of them moved immediately.

Then Abbie stood.

"I'll ask about permits tomorrow," she said.

Michael rose too.

"I'll measure the space."

They both smiled at the practicality of it.

Abbie closed the notebook.

"It's too nice to go straight home," she said lightly.

Michael looked up.

"No."

She hesitated only briefly.

"Would you like to walk again?"

He didn't hesitate.

"Yes."

They left the square together, turning toward the river without discussion.

The towpath stretched ahead in pale afternoon light. The water moved quietly beside them, sunlight breaking against its surface.

They walked close from the beginning this time.

After a few minutes, Michael's hand brushed against hers.

Neither commented.

The second time it happened, he let his fingers curl slightly.

Abbie turned her hand over, and he took her hand in his.

They did not look at each other immediately.

They continued walking as if nothing unusual had occurred.

Michael's grip was steady but not possessive. Abbie felt no urgency, no uncertainty, only the quiet rightness of contact chosen rather than accidental.

After a while she said, softly, "We're very brave today."

Michael gave the faintest smile.

"Yes."

They walked nearly half an hour before stopping at a small bench overlooking the river. A narrowboat drifted slowly past, its wake spreading gently toward the bank.

Abbie opened her bag and pulled out a small parcel wrapped in wax paper.

"I brought sandwiches," she said.

"Prepared as always."

She handed him one.

After a few bites of his sandwich, Michael looked at her. "I should have said something."

"When?"

"Years ago."

Abbie studied him.

"You were shy."

"I was."

"So was I."

He blinked, surprised.

"You were?"

"Yes."

She smiled.

"I wondered why the handwriting in my margins never spoke to me."

He exhaled, half laugh, half disbelief.

"I thought I was subtle."

"You were," she said. "Very."

Silence settled again, but it felt full rather than empty.

The river moved steadily below them.

"I don't want to be subtle now," Michael said at last.

Abbie felt her throat tighten unexpectedly.

"I don't want you to be," she replied.

He reached for her hand again, not tentatively this time.

They sat like that for several long moments, watching the water.

When they finally stood to walk back toward town, they kept looking at each other and each time they caught each other's glance, they smiled.

Near the edge of the market, where the towpath gave way to stone, they slowed.

"Well," Abbie said softly.

"Well," he echoed.

Michael could feel the warmth of her even before he

moved. He lifted his hand and slowly brushed his fingers gently along her cheek. This time he did not hesitate.

Abbie leaned into the touch fully, her breath caught, and when he bent toward her, she met him halfway.

The first brush of his lips was careful, but the second was not. It deepened, becoming more passionate, his hand sliding from her cheek to the curve of her jaw, and her fingers tightening slightly in his coat.

When they finally drew back, neither moved away.

Michael rested his forehead lightly against hers.

"I should have done that years ago," he murmured.

Abbie smiled, her hand still resting against his chest.

"You're doing it now."

He kissed her once more, and when they stepped apart, the air between them felt changed in a way that could not be undone.

"That," Abbie said softly, "was not subtle."

"No," he agreed.

"Tomorrow," she said.

"Yes," he replied.

But now the word held promise.

They parted slowly, each turning toward home with the unmistakable knowledge that something long unfinished had finally begun.

When Abbie walked away, the notebook felt heavier in her bag, not from weight, but from purpose.

Michael remained at the table a moment longer.

For years after Janet died, decisions had felt unnecessary.

Now, one had arrived without effort.

He finished his drink and looked once more at the place in the market where a small wooden stall might stand.

The idea no longer felt like a memory of school fairs.

It felt like the future, and for the first time in a long while, that felt entirely right.

CHAPTER 19

Abby

Abbie did not turn on the radio when she entered the house.

She wanted the quiet to just sit and relax with her thoughts.

Her fingers rose to her lips without thinking. She could still feel the weight of his kiss there, and the warmth of his lips.

She sat in the chair by the window, letting the memory return with the way he had said her name, and how his lips had felt on hers.

She closed her eyes and Edward's face came to mind gently, without ache.

"I loved you," she whispered. "And I still do."

She let the truth settle within her, and then she added, softly, "But I am not finished living."

The permission she had tentatively given herself the night before now felt solid.

She pictured walking beside Michael again, not as a memory returned, but as a future unfolding.

She smiled, and for the first time, she did not feel divided between past and present. Instead, she felt whole.

MICHAEL

Michael stood at the window longer than usual.

He had not intended to kiss her with so much passion, and he had not expected the way she had kissed him back and the how it made him want more.

He ran a hand through his hair, half-laughing under his breath.

"Thirteen," he said softly. "And now closing in on seventy."

He thought of the boy who had hidden behind margin notes, and now of the man who had finally stepped forward.

He sat at his desk and pulled a scrap of paper toward him.

For once, he did not write a message for her, be wrote one for himself.

Say it.

He folded it carefully.

She had leaned toward him as if she had been waiting. He would not return to silence, not now.

He looked out into the darkened street.

Tomorrow, he thought, and this time the word carried anticipation instead of habit.

CHAPTER 20

MICHAEL

Michael arrived at the market early again, not just because it was his habit, but this time because he couldn't wait to see Abbie again.

The square was quiet, pale morning light resting against the stones. He stood near their usual table, hands in his coat pockets, feeling an unfamiliar but welcome nervousness.

When Abbie appeared at the edge of the square, she smiled when she saw him.

"Good morning."

"Good morning."

They sat, and for a moment, they simply looked at one another, and yesterday's kiss hovered gently between them.

Abbie wrapped her hands around her tea.

"You're very quiet," she said.

"I am."

She waited.

Michael had practiced the words in his head more than

once the night before, but now they felt simpler than he expected.

"I loved you," he said.

Abbie blinked.

He did not look away.

"I loved you then...at school. I didn't know how to say it. I didn't even know how to do anything about it."

The market began to stir around them, vendors lifting shutters and unloading their crates.

He continued. "I thought writing in the margins was brave, but it wasn't. It was safe and I forced my own anonymity."

Abbie's fingers tightened slightly around her cup.

"I didn't want to be safe yesterday," he said.

Silence stretched between them but it wasn't uncomfortable.

"I don't expect you to have felt the same," he added gently. "You didn't know."

Abbie's eyes were bright, but not with tears.

"You were kind," she said.

"I was in love."

He said it plainly.

Abbie let out a slow breath.

"I didn't know," she said softly.

"I know."

She set her cup down.

"But I do know something now."

He waited.

"I've been falling in love with you," she said carefully. "Since that first morning tea. Maybe even before that, without realizing."

Michael felt the words land deeper than any he had rehearsed.

"It's different," she continued. "It's choosing to allow myself to love someone else."

The market noise grew louder around them, but neither moved.

Michael reached for her hand across the table, and this time there was no hesitation at all.

"I love you, Abbie."

She held his gaze.

"And I love the man you are now," she said softly. "Very much."

They sat there in the middle of the waking market, hands joined, the ordinary world continuing without noticing that something extraordinary had been spoken plainly between them.

After a moment, Abbie laughed quietly.

"Well," she said, "that simplifies things."

Michael smiled.

"Yes. It does."

They stood slowly from the table.

Abbie adjusted her scarf, though it did not need adjusting.

Michael stepped closer, because distance suddenly felt unnecessary.

"So," she said softly.

"So," he echoed, and they both laughed.

Michael reached for her hand and drew her gently toward him.

He kissed her, and her hands rose naturally to rest against his chest, then higher, one at his shoulder, the other touching the back of his neck.

The kiss deepened, with familiarity already forming. They had the steadiness of people who had waited long enough.

When they parted, Abbie smiled, a smile that made him feel both young and completely himself.

"That was not subtle either," she murmured.

"I'm not trying to be," he replied.

She kissed him again, and he laughed softly against her lips. Abbie stepped back at last, though she did not let go of his hand immediately.

"See you in the morning," she said.

"I'll be here," he answered.

Michael stood watching her until she disappeared around the corner of the square, his mouth still curved in quiet disbelief.

Seventeen had never kissed her.

Closing in on seventy had.

And he intended to keep doing so.

CHAPTER 21

MICHAEL

The wood smelled like rain and sawdust.

Michael stood beside the small frame that would become their stall, measuring tape stretched between his hands. The boards leaned against the wall of the market storage shed, waiting to be assembled into something useful. He liked the feeling of materials becoming purpose.

Abbie arrived a few minutes later, carrying two cups of tea.

"I thought we might need encouragement," she said.

Michael accepted one.

"Thank you."

They stood side by side, looking at the simple wooden structure taking shape in front of them, four posts, a counter-height board, and a small roof frame waiting to be fastened into place.

It was not impressive, but it was theirs.

"Well," Abbie said, "it looks like the start of a stall."

Michael nodded.

"It's a good start."

He set the measuring tape down and reached for a screwdriver. The motion felt familiar in the way all practical tasks did, hands remembering before the mind needed to.

"You've done this before," Abbie observed.

"Post office repairs," he said. "Counters loosen over time."

"Everything does," she replied.

They worked slowly, without urgency.

Abbie held the edge of the board steady while Michael tightened the screws along the corner joint . She read instructions aloud from a folded sheet, occasionally laughing at how unnecessary they seemed.

The small wooden frame of the stall had begun to resemble something real, something that might, with enough care, hold more than just a kettle and cups.

"You're frowning at it," she said.

"I am considering its structural integrity."

"It's a coffee stall, not a cathedral."

Michael glanced up.

"All structures deserve respect."

She laughed softly.

The sound seemed to make him work more carefully, as though the stakes had risen. When he finished, he straightened, and for a moment they stood very close in the narrow space between stacked boards and the half-built counter.

"You have sawdust on your sleeve," she said.

"Do I?"

"Yes."

She brushed it away gently, her fingers lingering longer than necessary.

He caught her hand before she could pull it back.

"Thank you," he said quietly.

"For the sawdust?"

"For being here."

The simplicity of it made her breath hitch slightly.

Before she could overthink it, he leaned down and kissed her.

She smiled against his mouth.

"We're meant to be working," she murmured.

"We are."

He kissed her again anyway, softer this time, as if confirming that he could.

She let her hand slide up along his arm.

"You are not very disciplined," she said.

"I am selectively disciplined."

She laughed again.

A vendor passing by paused. "Starting something new?" he asked.

"Yes, a tea and coffee stall." Abbie said.

The vendor smiled.

"Good," he replied, and continued on.

Michael felt the quiet approval settle warmly.

They worked for another hour, measuring, adjusting, fastening the roof frame into place. Each time they passed tools back and forth, their fingers touched. Once, he steadied her at the waist when she stepped backward without looking.

When at last they stepped back to look at the finished structure, Abbie felt an unexpected swell of pride.

"It's perfect and it's ours." she said.

Michael studied it too.

It was simple, small, and sturdy.

"Yes," he agreed. "It's ours."

Abbie reached into her bag, sliding a long piece of foam board out. She nailed it carefully to the front side of the stall.

Michael read the hand painted words:

The Second Cup

He smiled.

"That's the right name."

"I thought so," she said.

Michael reached into his pocket for a marker and wrote on a scrap of paper.

He handed it to her.

Abbie opened it.

Open soon.

She laughed.

"That sounds official."

Michael shrugged.

"I was a postmaster."

They stood together in front of the stall for a moment, not speaking.

Abbie placed the biscuit tin beside the stack of cups.

Michael adjusted the position of the counter until it sat square against the stones.

Abbie handed him a note.

Michael opened it.

Proud of us.

He folded it carefully and placed it in his pocket.

"Yes," he said. "Me too."

The afternoon light slipped across the wood, warming the surface of the counter.

Michael rested his hand there for a moment and the stall felt solid beneath his palm. For the first time since the idea had appeared between them at the market table, he allowed himself to imagine the morning when the window would open, steam would rise into the air, and people would gather for warmth and conversation. He could see it clearly and suspected Abbie could too.

They stood beside the stall longer than necessary.

Abbie adjusted the small handwritten sign, then looked toward the river.

"It's too early to part," she said lightly.

Michael felt the same.

"Would you... like to come to my place for tea?" he asked.

The invitation felt larger than the words.

Abbie hesitated only a moment.

"I would."

His flat was small and orderly, a reflection of years of habit. He suddenly saw it through her eyes as she stepped inside.

"It smells like polish," she said.

"I cleaned."

"I can tell."

He removed his coat and took hers gently, hanging it beside his own.

The intimacy of the gesture made his pulse shift.

"I'll put the kettle on," he said.

She wandered slowly through the sitting room while he filled it, pausing at the small bookshelf, at the framed photograph on the mantel.

He joined her there.

"That was Janet," he said quietly.

"She looks kind."

"She was."

She touched his hand.

"I'm glad you had her."

He exhaled, relieved in a way he hadn't expected.

"And Edward?" he asked.

"He was a good man." she said.

They stood in shared understanding, not comparing or replacing, but acknowledging the difference.

The kettle clicked and they moved to the kitchen, standing close at the counter while he poured.

There was no market noise here and no passing vendors to distract them.

Just the quiet of a home holding two people who no longer intended or wanted to be alone.

When she reached for her cup, he caught her wrist gently and drew her closer instead.

The kiss this time was unhurried.

He slid one hand along her waist, and she stepped fully into him without hesitation.

When they parted, she rested her forehead briefly against his chest.

"I didn't think I would feel like this again," she admitted.

"Neither did I."

He brushed a strand of hair from her cheek.

"You deserve to."

"So do you."

They moved to the sitting room with their tea, settling side by side on the sofa rather than opposite one another.

Her shoulder rested against his naturally.

At one point, she turned her face toward his and kissed him again.

The afternoon light shifted slowly across the floor.

When she finally stood to leave, it felt less like departure and more like continuation.

"I'll see you tomorrow," she said.

"Yes."

And now tomorrow meant something entirely different than it had weeks before.

CHAPTER 22

Abbie arrived at the market, the sun was just barely up, with the air holding that deep morning cold that made breath visible. The square felt larger without the usual movement of people, the stalls standing silent like closed books.

She saw the wooden stall immediately.

The Second Cup.

The sign looked smaller in the early light, but somehow more real.

Michael was already there.

He stood behind the counter, adjusting the kettle with careful attention, as if it were a delicate instrument rather than an ordinary object.

Abbie felt something settle warmly in her chest.

"Good morning," she said.

Michael looked up, relief crossing his face so quickly it might have been missed by anyone else.

"Good morning."

She stepped behind the counter beside him.

"Everything ready?" she asked.

"I think so."

She set the biscuit tin in its place and lined up the cups again, though they were already straight.

"You're early," Michael said.

"So are you."

They smiled.

The small space of the stall felt unexpectedly comfortable, just wide enough for the two of them to stand without crowding, close enough that their hands touched when they reached for the same stack of cups.

Neither commented.

The kettle began to hum.

Abbie looked out across the empty market.

"I used to love the moment before students arrived," she said. "The classroom felt full of possibility."

Michael nodded.

"The post office felt like that when I unlocked the door."

They stood quietly, listening to the kettle build toward boiling.

A vendor crossed the square carrying crates and waved.

"Opening today?" he called.

"Yes," Abbie replied.

"Good," he said, continuing on.

The kettle clicked off.

Abbie poured the first two drinks.

She handed one to Michael.

He accepted it carefully.

"For staff," she said.

Michael smiled.

"Best customers."

They stood behind the counter together, sipping tea, watching the market wake.

The first customer arrived sooner than Abbie expected, an older man with a wool cap pulled low over his ears.

"Morning," he said.

"Morning," Abbie replied.

"Coffee, please."

Michael poured while Abbie reached for a cup.

The rhythm came easily.

Milk.

Lid.

Coins exchanged.

"Thank you," the man said, walking away.

Abbie let out a small breath.

"We've done it," she said.

Michael nodded.

"Yes."

More customers followed, and Abbie noticed Michael writing on a cup before handing it across the counter.

She didn't ask what it said, she didn't need to.

The market filled with the soft sounds of morning, their stall kettle boiling, quiet conversation, the scrape of coins, and laughter drifting from nearby vendors.

Abbie realized she was not thinking about what to do next; she was simply doing it, and Michael was beside her.

At one point, their hands reached for the same cup and Abbie laughed.

"You first," she said.

Michael handed her the cup and gave her a quick kiss.

The moment passed without comment, but something in Abbie's chest shifted again, deeper this time.

When the first quiet lull arrived, Abbie stepped back from the counter and looked at the small wooden stall, the cups stacked neatly, the biscuit tin open, the hand painted sign nailed to the front.

Michael followed her gaze.

"Well," he said.

"Well," she agreed.

He reached into his pocket and slid a folded note across the counter.

Abbie opened it.

Glad you're here.

She looked up at him, smiling.

"I am too," she said.

And in that moment, standing together in the small space of *The Second Cup*, Abbie understood something she hadn't yet named.

This was no longer just companionship. This was the beginning of love, the quiet kind that arrived not with thunder, but with the steady warmth of morning tea shared across a wooden counter.

CHAPTER 23

The first day of *The Second Cup* left Abbie pleasantly tired.

They had sold nearly everything. The biscuit tin sat empty. The kettle had worked without protest. Three different customers had returned for a second drink.

Michael had smiled more than she had ever seen him smile.

As they packed up the last of the cups, Abbie reached out and took his hand.

"Would you like to come for supper? I've something in the slow cooker." she asked, trying to sound casual.

Michael paused, just enough for her pulse to notice.

"I would," he said.

Her house smelled of rosemary and onions when they stepped inside.

"I put it on before we opened," she said, slipping off her coat. "Just in case the day ran long."

"What is it?"

"Lamb and vegetables. Nothing impressive."

"It smells wonderful."

She smiled at the approval in his voice.

The small kitchen felt warmer than usual with him in it. He leaned against the counter while she lifted the lid from the slow cooker, steam rising between them.

"It's been a long time since I've cooked for someone," she admitted.

Michael stepped closer.

"It's been a long time since someone's cooked for me."

The intimacy of that landed quietly.

They ate at her small wooden table, lamb, carrots, and potatoes softened into comfort food. The conversation was easy at first as they talked about the stall, customers, and whether they needed more cups.

But beneath it there was a new awareness.

After supper, Michael insisted on washing the plates.

"You cooked," he said.

She stood beside him anyway, drying what he handed her.

The kitchen light was softer now, and the world outside her window had darkened into evening.

"You were wonderful today," she said.

"So were you."

He turned, drying his hands slowly on a tea towel.

"Would you like to sit?" she asked.

They moved to the sitting room.

Abbie lit a small lamp instead of the overhead light. The room shifted into a dim glow. She chose something simple to watch, an old documentary neither had seen. His arm rested along the back of the cushions at first. Then, gradually, it settled around her shoulder as she leaned into him, feeling the warmth of his body through his shirt.

As the program murmured in the background, Abbie became aware of the slow rhythm of his breathing, and of the way his thumb traced small, absent circles along her upper arm.

She turned her face toward him.

He was already looking at her.

The kiss began gently, but it did not end there. Her hand slid upward, fingers threading into his hair. His hand moved from her shoulder to her waist, drawing her fully against him. She felt her feelings deepening and stirring, and she shifted closer without hesitation.

When he pulled back, it was only far enough to search her face. "Are you certain?" he asked softly.

"Yes," she said.

His hand moved along her back, slow and deliberate, learning the shape of her through fabric.

She felt heat rise to her cheeks as she grew more and more aware of him. They kissed again, deeper and lingering.

When his hand slipped briefly along her side, resting at her hip, she did not pull away, but drew him closer.

The air in the room felt warmer now.

The television had long since stopped being relevant.

After a long moment, Michael rested his forehead against hers.

"I don't want to rush you," he said quietly.

"You aren't," she replied.

But they both understood the threshold they stood near.

Abbie drew back just slightly, brushing her fingers along his cheek.

They remained on the sofa, touching, kissing softly, hands exploring only as far as comfort allowed. The desire was there, unmistakable, mature, and patient.

When at last they eased apart, it was not from reluctance.

It was from choice.

She rested her head against his shoulder, and he held her there, steady.

"Next time," she said softly.

"Yes," he answered.

And the promise in it was warm rather than urgent.

They sat like that until the lamp burned low and the night settled fully around the house.

CHAPTER 24

MICHAEL

The second morning at *The Second Cup* felt easier.

Michael unlocked the stall while the sky was still pale, his hands moving through the small routines they had already begun to learn. kettle filled, cups stacked, and the counter wiped.

He noticed, not for the first time, that he no longer thought of the market as somewhere he went, but as somewhere he arrived.

Abbie appeared a few minutes later, carrying a small paper bag.

"I brought scones," she said.

Michael smiled.

"Excellent decision."

She set the bag beside the biscuit tin and began arranging cups without needing to be asked.

The movement between them felt practiced already, as well as comfortable.

The kettle clicked on.

Abbie glanced toward him.

"You look happy," she said.

Michael considered that.

"I am," he replied.

She nodded, as if confirming something she had suspected.

The first customers arrived in twos and threes, drawn by the warmth of the stall and the smell of coffee drifting into the cold air.

Michael poured drinks while Abbie greeted people by name when she could, or by warmth when she couldn't.

"Cold morning," someone said.

"Warmer now," Abbie replied.

Michael watched her move easily through the small conversations, bracelets catching the morning light.

He realized, with quiet certainty, that the stall worked because she was there.

During a lull, he picked up a cup and uncapped a marker.

The word came without effort.

Begin again.

He handed the cup to a woman waiting at the counter.

She read it, smiled, and held the cup a little more carefully as she walked away.

Abbie noticed.

"That one felt important," she said.

"Yes," Michael replied.

They stood together in the quiet that followed.

Abbie reached into her bag and slid a folded note toward him.

Michael opened it.

Still time.

He laughed softly.

"You've been saving that one."

"Maybe."

Michael folded the note and placed it in his pocket.

Abbie broke a scone in half and handed a piece to Michael.

"For energy," she said.

"Necessary."

They ate in companionable silence.

Michael found himself thinking about how easily the days now moved from morning into afternoon without the long empty spaces that once stretched between.

When Abbie stepped away briefly to speak with a vendor, Michael felt the absence immediately, and he felt relieved when she stood beside him again.

They worked in an easy rhythm, but something had shifted.

When Michael reached past her for the tin of sugar, his hand settled briefly at her waist instead of the counter.

Abbie smiled up at him.

"You're distracting me," she said quietly.

"I'm attempting to help."

"That is not helping."

He smiled and leaned down to kiss her lightly before stepping back to serve the next customer.

Later, when the queue thinned, she caught him watching her as she laughed with a returning customer.

"What?" she asked.

"Nothing."

"That wasn't nothing."

"I like seeing you happy."

The simplicity of it made her smile.

At one point she brushed a crumb from his lip, and

instead of withdrawing, she kissed him there, quick and unembarrassed.

"Public display," he murmured.

"It's our stall," she replied.

Michael realized something then: love did not always arrive like a letter marked urgent, sometimes it arrived like regular post.

He poured another cup of coffee and set it on the counter beside Abbie's tea.

They stood there together, watching the market move through another ordinary morning.

And Michael knew, without needing to say it aloud, that he did not want to run *The Second Cup* without her.

***

At the end of the day as they packed away the kettle, Michael caught her hand and turned her gently toward him.

"We did well," he said.

"Yes."

He kissed her, slower than earlier, deeper, and she felt the kiss settle lower in her body.

The awareness lingered, long after she arrived back home.

CHAPTER 25

MICHAEL

That evening they decided to cook a meal together at her house.

They had chosen something simple, fish pie, crust browned just enough.

Abbie stood beside him in the kitchen, sleeves rolled, bracelets pushed back.

She stepped behind him to reach the cupboard and brushed fully against his back.

He turned slowly.

"You did that deliberately."

"Yes."

He kissed her then, and her hands moved beneath his jacket, feeling the warmth of him through his shirt. His fingers slid along her waist, settling at the small of her back.

The oven timer chimed.

Neither moved.

Finally, she laughed softly against his mouth.
"The fish pie."
"Right."
They separated reluctantly.

ABBIE

After supper they did not turn on the television.

They sat closer than before.

His hand resting possessively, comfortably at her hip.

Their conversation slowed, and Abbie traced the line of his collar with one finger.

"You look at me differently now," she said.

"I feel differently now."

"How?"

"Like I am no longer waiting."

The words landed between them.

She leaned in and kissed him, slower and deeper than she had before.

This time when his hand moved, it did not stop at her waist. It explored, learning the shape of her more fully.

She responded without hesitation, and when he pulled back, it was only enough to ask again, softly:

"Are you certain?"

She did not answer with words, but stood, and held out her hand.

"Come with me."

The invitation was quiet and intentional with meaning that could not be misunderstood.

Michael stood slowly.

At her bedroom door, she paused.

He brushed his thumb along her cheek.

"You don't have to prove anything," he said gently.

"I'm not," she replied as she closed the door behind them. "I want you here."

CHAPTER 26

ABBIE

A bbie woke before the light fully reached the curtains. For a moment she did not move but then became aware first of warmth and then of the weight of the steady presence of an arm resting across her waist, Michael's arm.

She turned her head slowly and looked at him.

He was still asleep; his face softened in a way she had never seen in daylight. One hand lay open against the pillow between them, his breathing even and unguarded.

She reached up and traced the faint line at the corner of his eye with one fingertip.

His breath shifted and his eyes opened slowly and he gazed at her.

"Good morning," he murmured.

Her heart did something quiet and certain in her chest.

"Good morning."

They remained still, looking at one another as if confirming that the night had been real.

He brushed his thumb lightly along her side. She leaned forward and kissed him gently.

It was different than the night before, and when she pulled back, he smiled.

"You're still here," he said.

"So are you."

He shifted slightly closer, resting his forehead against hers.

There was no awkwardness, no hesitation, and no regret between them.

After a while she slipped from the bed.

"I'll make tea," she said.

"I'll make it," he answered, already pushing himself up.

She watched him cross the room, pulling on his shirt. The domestic ordinariness of it felt unexpectedly intimate.

In the kitchen, sunlight filtered through the window above the sink.

He stood at the kettle, hair slightly rumpled, sleeves rolled back.

She came up behind him and wrapped her arms around his waist.

He stilled for a moment, then leaned back into her.

"I like this," he said quietly.

"So do I."

She rested her cheek against his back.

The kettle clicked, but he ignored it and he turned in her arms, cupping her face briefly before pressing a slow, deep kiss to her mouth.

They ate toast at the small kitchen table, knees touching beneath it.

He reached for the marmalade at the same time she did.

He covered her hand with his and held it there for a second longer than necessary.

"You're certain?" he asked softly.

She met his gaze.

"Yes."

The word carried no tremor.

"I've never felt rushed," she added. "Not once."

He nodded, something in his shoulders easing.

"And you?" she asked.

"I feel…" He paused, searching.

"Content."

The word surprised them both.

She smiled.

"Yes," she said. "That's it. I'll add happy to that as well."

They finished breakfast slowly, neither eager to disturb the quiet.

When he rose to leave later, he did not step toward the door immediately.

Instead, he took her hands.

"I don't want to lose this," he said.

"You won't."

"How do you know?"

"Because we're choosing it."

He exhaled in relief, leaned forward and kissed her once more.

When he finally stepped outside into the morning air, she remained at the doorway watching him walk down the path.

He turned once before the gate to smile and wave at her.

She lifted her hand in reply and smiled as she closed the door to prepare for the day at the market.

The rhythm of the stall settled quickly. Abbie no longer needed to think about where things belonged. Cups stacked themselves beneath her hands. The kettle's timing became familiar. The biscuit tin found its place beside the napkins as naturally as if it had always lived there.

Abbie arrived to find Michael already there, adjusting a new wooden sign at the front of the stall.

"Crooked?" she asked.

"Possibly."

She tilted her head, then straightened it slightly.

"Better."

Michael nodded.

"Yes."

They stood together for a moment, looking at the small wooden counter, the new sign and the steam from the kettle rising into the cool air.

The Second Cup.

The market bells rang the hour.

Abbie poured tea while Michael arranged cups.

A familiar quiet settled between them, not silence, but comfort.

"Do you remember school mornings?" she asked.

Michael smiled.

"Yes."

"They always felt like beginnings," she said.

"They were."

Abbie handed him his tea.

"For staff," she said again.

Michael chuckled.

"Best customers."

They drank slowly, watching vendors set up their stalls and greet one another across the square.

Abbie realized something then. The mornings no longer

felt like something she filled with activity, but like somewhere she belonged. She belonged beside Michael.

A woman approached the stall.

"Coffee, please."

"Of course," Abbie said.

Michael poured while she prepared the cup.

The exchange felt simple and right.

When the woman walked away, Abbie leaned lightly against the counter.

"I'm glad we did this," she said.

Michael nodded.

"So am I."

The kettle hummed again.

Abbie reached into her pocket and pulled out a folded piece of paper.

She placed it on the counter between them.

Michael opened it.

Here we are.

He looked up at her.

"Yes," he said.

Michael picked up a marker and wrote carefully on the side of an empty cup.

He handed it to Abbie.

She turned it toward the light.

Begin again.

Abbie smiled and he gave her a quick kiss before the day unfolded around them as the market filled with people. Abbie set the cup beside the kettle, and Michael rested his hand briefly over hers as she smiled up at him.

The Second Cup stall opened to the market, and together they welcomed the day.

CHAPTER 27

MICHAEL

The next morning, they walked to the stall together. Abbie carried the biscuit tin, he carried the kettle, their free hands clasped together.

"You're humming," she said lightly.

"I am not."

"You are."

He stopped.

"...Possibly."

She smiled in a way that made it impossible to pretend otherwise. He smiled back at her, a sheepish sort of smile that only made her smile more.

The first customers arrived before the water in the kettle had fully boiled.

A small boy tugged at his mother's sleeve near the counter.

"Why are they smiling like that?" he asked, far too loudly.

His mother flushed and shushed him.

But Abbie laughed.

"Because we've had a good morning and we're happy." she said.

The boy studied them suspiciously, then nodded as if satisfied with the explanation.

Michael leaned closer to her as he handed over change.

"I suppose we are obvious," he murmured.

"Perhaps a little."

Throughout the morning, their movements around one another were unspoken choreography.

When he reached for the stack of cups, she shifted automatically to make room.

When she stepped back, his hand found her waist without looking.

Once, when no customers stood waiting, he bent to kiss her quickly.

She pressed her hand to his chest afterward, laughing quietly.

"Someone will see."

"They already have."

That did not seem to trouble either of them.

Near midday, an elderly gentleman who had visited on opening day returned.

"Business is brisk," he observed.

"We're grateful," Michael replied.

The man looked between them thoughtfully.

"You've settled into it quickly together. You make a good team."

"Yes," Abbie said softly.

The man nodded once, as if understanding more than was spoken.

"Well," he said, accepting his cup, "it suits you both."

After he left, Michael stood still for a moment.

"It does," he said.

Abbie met his eyes.

"Yes."

By afternoon, the market grew busier.

At one point, as she leaned forward to hand a customer their drink, Michael watched the sunlight catch in her hair, and had the sudden, overwhelming awareness that his feelings for her was not temporary.

When the crowd thinned, he turned to her and kissed her again openly.

"We should be subtle," she whispered.

"I have retired from subtlety."

She laughed.

Later, as they packed away the last of the cups, a woman who had purchased tea twice that morning paused.

"You two make it feel warm here," she said.

Abbie blinked.

"We hope so."

"It's not just the tea," the woman replied, as she continued on her way.

Michael looked at Abbie.

"Well," he said quietly.

"Well."

They closed the stall together, their movements unhurried.

As they walked toward the river afterward, their hands found each other naturally.

CHAPTER 28

ABBIE

The morning had begun lightly.

The square was already warm with sunlight, and Michael had just leaned over the counter to kiss her quickly, before turning to serve the next customer.

"Professional conduct," she had murmured, smiling.

"I have retired from subtlety," he had replied. "Maybe I should have that printed on a shirt."

She was still smiling when she saw her.

Laurie Talbot, Edward's sister.

Laurie slowed as she approached the stall, her gaze landing not on the sign, but on them.

On Michael standing slightly too close and Abbie's hand still resting on his arm.

"Abbie," Laurie said.

The warmth in Abbie's face cooled and she stiffened.

"Laurie," she answered.

Michael stepped back half a pace.

"Good morning," he said.

Laurie nodded at him, then looked at Abbie again.

"I've heard about this little venture."

"We opened recently," Abbie said.

"Yes." Laurie's eyes narrowed and flicked toward Michael and then back to Abbie, her lips pressed together tightly, "I can see that."

Michael said nothing.

Abbie kept her voice even. "Would you like tea...on the house?"

Laurie hesitated, then nodded. "Yes, thank you...with milk and sugar."

Michael prepared it in silence.

As he handed it over, Laurie spoke to Abbie again.

"It hasn't been that long."

Abbie's fingers tightened slightly around the counter's edge.

"It's been several years," she said softly.

Laurie's gaze sharpened. "And Edward?"

Abbie lifted her chin.

"I loved him," she said simply.

Laurie's lips pinched. "I just think you are not respecting his memory," she said coldly, "and I don't think it's right for you to forget him."

Michael stepped forward then.

"No one is forgotten," he said. "Abbie will always remember Edward, just as I will always remember my wife Janet, and we'll share those memories together."

Laurie studied him and then Abbie.

"I suppose time moves differently for everyone." She turned and walked away without another word.

The space she left behind felt cooler.

MICHAEL

They worked the rest of the morning without incident, but the former happiness had been replaced by something else.

When they closed the stall and walked toward the river, Abbie's hand found his, but her grip was lighter.

After a while she said, "Do you think she thinks I am wrong for being with you?"

Michael stopped walking.

"I think she probably does. But I don't care what she believes."

But she did care. He could see it in her face.

"I don't want to seem unfaithful," she said softly.

"You aren't."

"But what if it looks like I've replaced him?"

The vulnerability in her voice struck him harder than Laurie's words had.

He stepped closer. "You haven't replaced anyone."

She blinked.

"Edward loved you," he continued. "Janet loved me. We both love them, and we are not pretending otherwise."

Abbie's eyes shimmered faintly.

"For a moment," she admitted, "I wondered if we've been selfish."

He cupped her face gently.

"Do you feel selfish?"

"No."

"Do you feel disloyal?"

"No."

"What do you feel?"

She hesitated only briefly.

"Alive."

The word landed between them with quiet power.

Michael exhaled.

"I loved Janet," he said. "I always will."

"I know."

"And loving you doesn't diminish that."

She closed her eyes.

"I loved Edward," she whispered. "But I am still here."

He leaned his forehead against hers.

"We are not erasing anyone," he said softly. "We are continuing our lives."

Her hands slid around his waist, holding him more firmly now.

"I don't want to apologize for this," she said.

"Then don't."

They stood there in the soft afternoon light, and after a moment, she said, "Promise me something."

"Anything."

"That if anyone questions us again, we answer kindly."

"We will."

"And we won't let it make us feel like we are doing something wrong."

His grip tightened slightly.

"We won't."

She kissed him then, and when they resumed walking, their hands were firmly intertwined.

CHAPTER 29

Michael

The stall closed earlier than usual.

A steady rain had driven the market thin by late afternoon, and Abbie had insisted they not linger unnecessarily.

"We'll be here tomorrow," she said.

They carried the kettle between them toward the small storage shed near the square.

When they finished locking everything away, the rain had softened into mist.

"Walk?" she asked.

"Yes."

The towpath shimmered faintly in the damp light. Boats rocked gently against their ropes.

After a while Abbie said, "We'll need a thicker awning before winter."

"Yes."

"And perhaps lanterns for when it grows darker earlier."

He nodded.

"And more cups," she added. "If today was any indication."

He glanced at her.

"You're planning ahead."

"I am."

"For how long?"

She smiled faintly.

"As long as it continues."

He studied her profile, the way the soft grey sky settled around her.

"I was thinking," he said slowly, "we might keep the stall open through Christmas."

She looked surprised.

"That's ambitious."

"People want warmth when it's cold."

Her eyes softened.

"Yes," she said. "They do."

They walked a few more steps.

"And next spring," she continued thoughtfully, "we could plant something in small pots along the counter."

"Flowers?"

"Yes."

He considered it.

"That would look nice."

The future slid naturally into their conversation.

They stopped near a bend in the river where the water widened.

The mist had thickened slightly, softening the edges of everything.

Abbie slipped her hand into his without looking.

He watched the slow movement of the river and understood something quietly, almost without noticing when the thought fully formed:

I do not want to walk home alone anymore.

Abbie leaned lightly against his arm.

"You're very quiet," she said.

"I'm thinking."

"About?"

He hesitated only briefly.

"About how easily this feels like... ours."

She did not pull away.

"It does," she agreed.

"I used to return to a house," he continued carefully. "Now I find myself thinking of being where you are, and I don't want to walk home alone anymore."

She tilted her head slightly and squeezed his hand.

"I like when you stay for supper," she said.

"So do I."

"And when you wake up there."

He felt warmth move through him.

"Yes."

The mist drifted lightly across the water.

"For a moment after Laurie left," Abbie said quietly, "I wondered if this might shrink under pressure."

"And?"

"It hasn't."

He turned to face her fully.

"It won't," he said.

She looked at him steadily.

"Do you ever think," she began, then paused.

"What?"

"That perhaps this is what was meant to happen all along?"

He considered that.

"I don't know about meant," he said honestly. "But I know about now."

She smiled.

"Now is enough."

He brushed his thumb gently across the back of her hand.

"Yes," he said. "It is."

They stood there together for several long moments, watching the river move.

Michael felt the simple awareness that his life had shifted from something contained to something shared.

When they finally turned back toward town, he did not release her hand.

And when they reached her gate, he did not step away immediately.

"Tea?" she asked.

"Yes."

The word came without hesitation, because he already knew.

He belonged where she was.

CHAPTER 30

Abbie

The house felt different. Abbie stood in the kitchen doorway and looked at the two cups sitting on the counter after Michael had left for the evening. She carried them to the sink and washed them carefully, as she always did.

She reached for one, his, intending to return it to the cupboard, but paused, and then she set it beside her own in its usual spot on the counter instead, both ready for the next time.

His laughter still seemed to echo faintly near the window. She moved slowly through the room, touching small things without meaning to, the back of the chair where he had sat, and the edge of the counter where he had leaned. She missed his presence.

She walked into the sitting room and lowered herself into the armchair and let her gaze drift to the mantel. Edward's photograph remained where it always had. She stood up again and walked over to it.

"I don't feel guilty," she said quietly.

The words were not defensive.

"I thought I might."

She touched the frame gently.

"You gave me many good years and I am grateful."

She stepped back and studied the room. It had been her alone for a long time,

sometimes lonely but often peaceful.

But now it felt as though it was waiting to be shared, waiting for another coat on the hook, and for two cups on the table.

She stood at the window and watched the faint light along the river path. She thought of Michael's hands steadying the stall frame, and of the way he looked at her when he believed she wasn't watching.

She turned off the lamp and climbed the stairs.

In the bedroom, she paused at the bedside table. His book lay where he had left it the night before. She picked it up, thumb resting briefly between the pages to mark his place, then set it back down where it belonged.

In the bathroom, his toothbrush rested beside hers. She didn't move it.

Back in the bedroom, she slipped beneath the duvet and reached automatically toward the space beside her, still warm from memory.

She smiled faintly into the darkness.

"I don't want you visiting," she murmured into the quiet room.

"I want you here, because we belong together."

The difference mattered.

CHAPTER 31

MICHAEL

They'd had a steady day at the stall the next day, but rain had returned lightly by evening. Not heavy enough to cancel the market, but steady enough to keep customers brief, so they packed up early again.

"Tea?" Abbie asked as they reached her gate.

"Yes," he said, as if there were no other possible answer.

Her kitchen glowed with lamplight when they stepped inside. She moved easily through the space now when he was there.

He hung his coat on the hook beside hers.

It no longer felt strange.

She filled the kettle, and he watched her move, the simple familiarity of it tightening something in his chest.

"Sit," she said.

He did.

The kettle clicked and the steam rose and she filled two cups.

She placed his in front of him without asking how he

liked it, but it was exactly right and that detail nearly undid him.

They sat opposite one another at the small table as rain tapped gently at the window, and for a few moments they said nothing.

Abbie wrapped her hands around her cup.

"You're thinking," she said.

"I am."

"Should I be concerned?"

"No."

He stood abruptly and moved to the cupboard above the sink.

She watched him, puzzled.

He reached up and brought down a third cup.

One she rarely used.

He placed it on the table beside theirs.

"We don't need three," she said lightly.

"No," he replied.

He moved her cup closer to his.

Then his closer to hers.

Leaving the third slightly apart.

He looked at her.

"The third cup is me when I go home to my flat. The other two, that's you and I in the same place, this house. I don't want to go home alone anymore."

She stilled.

"Michael—"

"I don't want to pack away my coat and walk back to a place that feels like it's waiting for something to happen, and nothing does because you aren't there with me."

He took a slow breath.

"This feels like where I belong...here with you."

The rain deepened slightly against the glass.

He met her eyes.

"I loved Janet. I always will."

"I know."

"But I do not want to spend the rest of my life visiting you."

Her breath caught.

He reached across the table and took her hands.

"Marry me, Abbie."

"I want to wake up here every morning," he continued. "I want to build the stall through winter and spring and every year after that. I want this table to be ours. I want... home to be where you are."

She blinked quickly.

"Michael."

"I am not asking because I am lonely. I am asking because I love you."

Tears slid quietly down her cheeks.

"You are very brave these days," she whispered.

"I am tired of being subtle."

That made her laugh through tears.

She stood then, walking around the table instead of answering from across it.

She took his face in her hands.

"Yes."

The word came without hesitation.

"Yes, I will marry you. I love you, Michael."

He closed his eyes briefly, relief flooding through him.

She kissed him, and when they parted, she rested her forehead against his.

"We should discuss where," she said.

He smiled faintly.

"Yes."

"You don't love your flat."

"No."

"You never really settled after Janet."

He shook his head.

"I sold the larger place after she died. The flat I have now... it was convenient."

She nodded.

"This house has already adjusted to you," she said quietly.

He glanced around.

His cup beside hers.

His book on the bedside table.

His toothbrush by the sink.

"Yes," he said.

"It would make sense," she continued, practical even now, "for you to move in here."

"It would."

"I don't want to leave this kitchen."

"Then don't."

He brushed his thumb gently across her cheek.

"I'll sell the flat."

"You're certain?"

"Yes."

She smiled through lingering tears.

"Then this is ours."

He kissed her again and she pulled him closer.

"Stay," she said.

"I'm not going anywhere."

She took his hand and led him toward the hallway.

The door to her bedroom—now *their* bedroom— closed softly behind them.

EPILOGUE

The morning had settled into its steady rhythm when Michael noticed the two men approaching the stall.

He recognized them before they reached the counter.

One tall and thoughtful, moving with the quiet attentiveness of someone used to watching the world carefully. The other also tall but broader in build, his expression curious but reserved, as if conversation were something he approached cautiously.

Michael had seen them both years before, standing at the post office counter on different mornings, sending letters to different places.

He remembered people that way.

"Good morning," Michael said.

The taller man smiled.

"Michael," he replied. "I thought that was you."

Andrew Collins.

Michael remembered the name as easily as if it had been written yesterday.

"It's nice to see you." Michael said.

The other man with him had not been as regular.

"Nigel," he said. "Nigel Walker."

Michael inclined his head in greeting.

Abbie glanced between them with interest, wiping the counter with a cloth.

"You know each other?" she asked.

"Post office," Andrew said. "Years ago."

Michael smiled.

"A familiar face," he said.

Andrew looked around the stall.

"This is new."

"It is," Abbie replied. "We've just opened. I'm Abbie."

Nigel studied the hand painted sign.

The Second Cup

Michael & Abbie Holmes

"I like the name of your stall, Abbie," he said.

"Thank you," Abbie said warmly.

"What can we get you?" Michael asked.

"Coffee," Andrew said.

"Tea," Nigel added.

Michael prepared the cups while Abbie poured and handed the drinks across the counter.

Andrew noticed the writing on his cup first.

He turned it slightly.

Still time.

His expression changed, not dramatically, just enough to suggest the words had landed somewhere meaningful.

Nigel glanced at his own cup.

Try anyway.

He exhaled softly through his nose, almost a laugh.

"That's... unexpectedly encouraging," he said.

Michael shrugged.

"Habit."

Andrew smiled into his coffee.

"Well," he said, "thank you."

They stood there a moment longer than customers usually did.

Abbie recognized the feeling, people sometimes needed a minute with warmth before moving on.

"Cold morning," she said.

"Not as cold as yesterday," Nigel replied.

Andrew nodded toward the river path.

"Nice place for a stall."

"We thought so," Michael said.

Andrew lifted his cup slightly in acknowledgment.

"Glad to see you again, Michael."

"And you."

Nigel did the same.

"Good luck with the stall," he said.

"Thank you," Abbie replied.

They walked away together, cups warming their hands as they crossed the square.

Abbie watched them go.

"Nice men," she said.

"Yes," Michael agreed.

He reached for the marker again, then paused.

"What?" Abbie asked.

"Nothing," he said.

But he was thinking about the words he had written on their cups and wondering why they had seemed the right words to write for both of the men.

Abbie slipped a small, folded note across the counter.

Michael opened it.

See?

He smiled.

"Yes," he said again.

Behind them, the kettle began to hum.

Michael leaned toward Abbie and pressed a quick, familiar kiss to her temple before reaching for the kettle again.

Abbie smiled and passed him another cup without looking, their movements easy and practiced now.

Across the square, Andrew and Nigel walked on, disappearing into the morning crowd.

Michael picked up the marker from beside the kettle and wrote a few quiet words along the side of the cup before sliding it toward the waiting customer.

The market carried on, and so did they.

Some people discover that love was waiting for them all along. Others are only just beginning to realize that there is still time.

Andrew's story begins that morning at The Second Cup when he reads the handwritten words on his paper cup. If you'd like to discover why "Still time" mattered to him, Andrew's story happens next in my full-length novel:
Where the Distance Ends
Book One of The Lives We Choose series.
Two hearts. One ocean. A love worth every mile.
For details, visit my website:
www.lizbrownbooks.com

ABOUT THE AUTHOR

Liz Brown writes cozy, heartwarming romance about second chances, meaningful journeys, and love that grows stronger with time. Her stories often celebrate later-in-life romance, exploring connection across distance, the comfort of home, and the courage it takes to begin again.

Inspired by travel, small towns, and the quiet moments that shape a life, Liz creates character-driven novels filled with warmth, humor, and hope.

She lives in Maine, where she writes with a favorite fountain pen nearby and far too many books within reach. When she isn't writing, she enjoys visiting England, collecting story ideas, and imagining the next chapter for her characters.

www.lizbrownbooks.com

instagram.com/lizbrownauthor

facebook.com/lizbrownauthor

tiktok.com/@lizbrownauthor